L. J. Cherry was born in Welwyn Garden City, but raised from a young age in Swansea. Taking a great interest in politics, history, and philosophy, his education took him to Oxford Brookes University. After graduating with a 2.1 in Politics and Philosophy, he moved to Brighton and spent the next five years working with students from troubled backgrounds and with mental health difficulties. Moving back to Swansea, whilst continuing his work with students, he acquired a diploma in existential counselling, studied psychology, and volunteered in his spare time supporting bereaved people with Cruse Bereavement Care. An admirer of existential philosophy, Liam has attempted to sew its ideas throughout this story. As a first-time author, Liam is excited to share this book with you and he hopes you enjoy reading it, as much as he enjoyed writing it.

I would like to dedicate this book to my beautiful wife, Leah. She has stood by me and endured all of my crazy schemes, such as writing a novel.

L.J. Cherry

NOTHING LEFT BEHIND

AUSTIN MACAULEY PUBLISHERS™

LONDON • CAMBRIDGE • NEW YORK • SHARJAH

A CIP catalogue record for this title is available from the British Library.

ISBN 9781398436381 (Paperback)
ISBN 9781398436398 (ePub e-book)

www.austinmacauley.com

First Published 2022
Austin Macauley Publishers Ltd®
1 Canada Square
Canary Wharf
London
E14 5AA

I am very grateful to Austin Macauley Publishers for seeing my vision and bringing my book to life. At a time when so many will not even consider new authors, Austin Macauley are bringing new and exciting authors into our libraries and book shops.

Table of Contents

Chapter 1 – The End Part 1

He walked into his house. This task was managed, with surprising ease – he walked to the door, inserted the key, turned it clockwise until he heard the familiar click of the lock, applied sufficient force on the handle and let himself in – he feared now he was getting all too close to sober. He went straight to the kitchen and shuffled in the alcohol cupboard for something, anything, to prevent such a catastrophe. He didn't need to stay inebriated for much longer, just enough to see him to the end. Vodka. A third of a bottle. *That'll do*, he thought. He brought the bottle to his lips and tilted it just enough for the liquid to slowly transport from the bottle into his stomach. He drank it in one go. There was a time, he thought fleetingly, when the taste of vodka would make him heave, make him reach for something to chase it with to remove the taste. Now, however, it tastes of nothing, his tongue was numb to vodka... to anything, actually. How he had punished his tongue, his mouth, his body, recently. He really was sobering up and he was desperate for the vodka to kick in and remove these truths from his mind.

Sitting on the sofa, he peered down at his hands. There were a few blood stains, some mud, a nasty cut. Tentatively bringing them to his face, they smelt of all-too-many things. He hadn't washed in days. He could feel it in his mouth. Dry. His tongue noticed the coating on his teeth, it was dense, carpet like. And then it found the spot where, until recently, one of his teeth had been. He felt now the punch that knocked it out. It was a good punch he had to admit. One, in any normal circumstances, he would have thoroughly deserved. But he thought then, and still does now, with what is coming does it matter? Does any of it really matter? Take what you can get, when you can get it, that's what he thought. There is no room for morals, for morality even, there is no good and evil anymore. It is all moot. Because, when faced with it… when you are face-to-face with the end, you have to grab all that you can get, before that scythe taps you on the head.

Footsteps upstairs. He listened as the creaking floorboard gave away his wife's path. The bathroom. Quiet. Then the groaning of the pipes as she turned on the tap. *Creak… creak… creak.* She was near the top of the stairs now. He stayed quiet, not daring to breathe. He knew, however, that she wouldn't come downstairs. She was terrified of him. A stranger, she said, in her own house. For a moment, he imagined what was going through her head, perhaps a quiet sobbing. In fact, sobbing was the only state he knew her in anymore. Gone was the anger, the hope, the disappointment. Now, to him, she was a walking sobbing machine. And then, warmth. The vodka was doing its job. The warmth filled his stomach, his chest, it climbed up his throat and into his head. *Creak, creak, creak.* She was back in bed.

It was time. He was hoping the alcohol would numb his emotions. He tried to swallow it down, but it was of no use, he felt the tear land on his hand. Then another. He gave up fighting it, the tears streamed down his face. He could taste the salt of them in his mouth, how nice it was to taste something, he thought for a fraction of a second. His hands were shaking, on the verge of hysterical. Then anger. *You will not dictate this*, he thought. 'You will not dictate this,' he whispered out loud through gritted teeth, 'I will decide my time.' For a moment, his mind deceived him, and he considered his wife's sadness upon seeing him in the morning. Twenty-four hours, he told himself, what does it matter if she is sad for twenty-four hours?

It was time. With his right hand, almost beyond his own control, he picked up a cushion and placed it against the left side of his head. His left hand then, shaking, pulled open the hidden draw under the sofa. Taking out the letters, he placed them on the coffee table. Then he unwrapped the newspaper and pulled it out. Heavier than he remembered, he felt the weight of the cold steel in his hands. He shook all over, violently now. This was it. It was time. With the cushion still in place, he brought the revolver up to it, aligned it with his temple, and squeezed on the trigger…

Chapter 2 – The Neighbour
Part 1

Thud... thud... thud. She recoiled on the sofa, squeezing herself against its arm, she clenched her knees into her chest and hid her pale face behind them. The pace of her heartbeat quickened as the sound seemed to tremble her whole body. *Thud... thud... thud.* Her nails pierced the skin of her shins; however the pain wasn't recognised by her brain. At first, and for only a fleeting second, excitement came over her, the excitement of "what could it be?" But it left her almost as soon as it came, her anxiety overwhelming every cell in her body. A cold shiver ran down her spine whilst her palms began to sweat. A tiny voice inside was screaming at her, but it was so faint, so quiet, no words were understood. In fact, all sound was drowned out now, the news on the television, the ticking of the clock on the wall, the regular drip of the tap in the kitchen, all blended into a distant white noise as the thuds dominated every sense.

THUD… THUD… THUD.

'Huh.' A sharp, fearful gasp, combined with an involuntary jump of her whole body. Then a whinny, terrified moan made its way out of her now quivering lips. She knew what she had to do. It was obvious to her, yet so alien at the same time. To any normal person this would be easy, simple, an everyday task. But to Eve, this was an event she feared happening every second. She knew too, what was out there. You see, she didn't feel safe inside her house, far from it, she just felt safer than outside her house. What it was, the bringer of the noise, was the world. The whole world. It was out there. Just outside, on her front porch. It haunted her. Mocked her. Stood there and waited. Its eyes pierced her through every window. It's sound screamed at her through cats screeching, lawnmowers mowing, the footsteps of joggers passing by. It waited to pounce on her as soon as she left. Like a hermit crab leaving its shell she became vulnerable outside that door. Fragile. Weak. She could be harmed in so many ways. She so rarely left, only when she had to. Once a week to see the doctor and, perhaps, once a fortnight when she had run out of all groceries.

THUD… THUD… THUD.

'Aah!' A slight scream this time combined with another jump. The screech of the letter box. 'Hello dear… I'm sure you are in, it's only me.' She could see now, from the sofa she was pressed into through the letter box into the world.

'Okay… okay… okay… okay… okay… okay,' Eve's mouth whispered slight encouragement to herself. Standing up, with shaking knees, she embarked on the long walk to the door. Clutching at the cabinet and wall to balance herself on the way, she eventually made it. Her heart was audible through her chest and with a slow, quivering breath, she precariously opened the door.

'Hello dear.' She heard the old woman's voice from beyond the door. 'Just had some leftover casserole I thought you'd like.' With a smile, she handed over the baking tray. Eve's thin, shaking arms took it off her, her wild fearful eyes didn't leave her neighbours face, staring at her as if a lion trying to gain entry and she quickly shut the door behind her without a word.

She survived. A deep breath. Eve placed the casserole in the kitchen, this wasn't her first casserole from her neighbour, and it was not her preferred meal. Last time she was so fearful the neighbour would smell the thing in Eve's bin, she forced it all into her churning stomach.

Sitting back on the sofa the ticking off the clock, the taps drip and the television all filled her ears once again with their sound and she relaxed, a little. Just at that time a most curious news story was being told, which brought all of Eve's fears rushing back again.

Chapter 3 – The Dragon Part 1

Joel gave himself ten seconds, a deep breath, attempting to mask his weariness, before walking through the front door. He was immediately pounced upon.

'Daddy! Daddy! Daddy!'

He spun her around and held her at his hip whilst she clung to his neck. He smiled. How his troubles seemed to melt away with her contagious smile.

'You're late, Daddy.'

Rayna, his wife, kissed him and handed him a cup of tea.

'He's not your daddy, silly!'

Rayna tickled her daughter until she was squirming in Joel's arm… it was all he could do to prevent the tea from spilling.

'I ran over today.' He sighed. 'It's been a long day.'

'Again?'

'It's been a long week.' Their eyes locked. 'Every week seems to be getting longer. There's something in the water, I can sense a difference at work.'

'You're tired. I can see it in your face.' Rayna's hand gently placed itself on his cheek. 'You sleep okay last night?'

'Not the best. But not the worst.' He kissed her forehead. 'I'll sleep better tonight.'

But probably not, he thought. The truth was he hadn't slept well for weeks. He had been plagued with anxiety provoking nightmares. He'd had nightmares before, but rare and sporadic. These were different. Each night, without fail, regular as clockwork, and deeply disturbing. In fact, they disturbed him to his core. But he didn't want to share them with his wife yet, he told himself he didn't want to worry her. But, honestly, he thought it would make them too real to say out loud. They only existed in his memory and he wanted to keep it that way, for now at least. Tonight would be no exception.

He sat beside his daughter, telling one of her favourite bedtime stories. In fact, if he was totally honest, it was his favourite bedtime story that she kindly allowed him to read to her most nights:

...and Sam told his mum, 'Mum, I saw a baby dragon under my bed.'

'There is no such thing as dragons, Sam, just ignore it,' said Mum. So, Sam ignored the dragon.

The next day, Sam saw the dragon again, but this time it was too big to fit under his bed. It walked past him in the hallway. 'Mum, I saw the dragon again!'

'I told you, there is no such thing as dragons, just ignore it and it'll go away.' So, Sam ignored the dragon.

The next day, Sam saw it in the bathroom, but he closed his eyes and said, 'There is no such thing as dragons.' When he opened them, the dragon was gone. He breathed a sigh of relief.

The next day, Sam went into his parents' bedroom to wake them up, and there was the dragon, in the corner of the room, even bigger than before. Now it was bigger than him. He closed his eyes, and repeated, 'There is no such thing as dragons. There is no such thing as dragons.' When he opened them, the dragon had disappeared. But Sam knew it would be back.

When he came home from school, the dragon was in the kitchen, it was nearly as tall as the room and its head as big as a bath. But his mum just walked around the dragon to make food. Did she not see it? *Sam thought. He closed his eyes… it disappeared. Sam's dad wasn't anywhere to be found. Sam asked his mum, 'Mum, where is Dad?'*

Sam's mum replied, 'Ignore the dragon, Sam, and it'll disappear.'

Sam was confused and asked his mum the same question, 'Mum, where has Dad gone?' But Sam's mum gave the same answer.

The next day Sam woke up to hear the walls of the house groaning. He got out of bed and noticed a dragon wing bulging through his door. He climbed on the wing and out of his room, he was now on top of the dragon's body, and it filled the whole house. The other wing was in the bathroom, the neck reached out into the kitchen, its head had burst out the front door and its tail filled his parents' bedroom. Sam walked on top of the dragon until he got out of the front door. Standing outside was his mother, defiantly facing away from the dragon. Angrily, Sam demanded, 'Mum, the dragon is real, can't you see it?' Reluctantly, his mother turned around. Sam looked at the dragon. He was scared, it was massive, it could eat him in one, but he turned to look at it right in the eye. The dragon looked back at him and raised his head on its long neck until it was looking down at Sam. Sam gulped. He could feel his hands shaking with fear, but he didn't look away. 'I can see you, dragon,' he whispered. The dragon stared at him. 'I can see you, dragon,' he said slightly louder. 'I can see you, dragon,' he said with a loud, stern voice. The dragon's neck shortened; its head shrunk. 'I can see you, dragon,' said Sam again. The dragon's body shrunk to half the size, its wings got smaller, its tail no longer reached his parents' bedroom. 'I can see you, dragon,' Sam said with more strength.

His mum came to his side and also said, 'I can see you, dragon.' The dragon became smaller, and smaller, and smaller with every chant. Eventually, the dragon

21

was so small it could fit in Sam's hand. He picked it up and put it in his pocket. Sam's mum hugged him. She said how brave he was and apologised for not believing him. She promised to never ignore a dragon again. The next day, when Sam returned from school with his dragon still in his pocket, he found his dad had returned.

Joel could hear the deep breathing of his daughter. Fast asleep. He was so engrossed in the story, he wondered how long she had actually been sleeping. He gave her a kiss on her head. 'Goodnight, my brave girl.' He closed the door gently behind him, leaving it ajar.

'How lucky that girl is, to have inherited your beauty,' he said, joining her in bed.

'You are a saint! I am lucky to have you. And she is very lucky to have you as her father,' Rayna responded, without a hint of irony, Joel noticed.

She feels lucky to have me? He pondered. He knew she meant it. So much humility did Rayna possess, that she wouldn't dare entertain the idea that Joel was the lucky one. They would be hard pressed to find a single person in the world who, seeing the two of them together, would conclude that Rayna was, in fact, the lucky one. Not even his own mother, god rest her soul, thought it. She would often tell Joel that he is "punching above his weight", and to marry her before she noticed!

He looked at her whilst considering this. His eyes were drawn to her long dark brown hair, her olive eyes, her golden skin. Her baggy bedtime T-shirt even exuded beauty when worn by her. In comparison, he looked… ordinary. He didn't think he was bad looking. But certainly not in Rayna's league. If she was the premiership, he was probably pushing for promotion in division three. He kept himself in good shape, forcing himself to the gym three mornings a week. He miraculously still had a full head of hair; despite the hairless fate he feared his father had passed on. He had watched as the bags under his eyes changed, first noticing them at the age of twenty-five, how they had grown through the years. So did the wrinkles on his forehead. He remembered his fright upon noticing wrinkle number one, and his desperate attempts to remove it. Nowadays, they number in the double figures, but he has embraced them, so he tells himself. They are his, a part of his unique face. He kept a tan most of the year round and pulled off a suit well. All-in-all, Joel had embraced his age, once he accepted times inevitability. There was a time when it caused him great anxiety. Every clock reminding him. Tick, tick, tick. Every second was another second gone, and they went so quickly. However, as he achieved and experienced, he lost touch with time, it seemed to pass by in the background as he was living. Only given small reminders of its persistent advance with a brand-new forehead wrinkle.

Passing up on the idea of reading, he was too tiresome for that tonight as his long drawn out yawn exposed. Kissing his wife goodnight, his contentment was interrupted by fleeting images of the nightmare to come. He physically shook them out of his head, and managed to fall asleep, it seemed, before his head even hit the pillow.

Chapter 4 – Anxiety

Eve: It's been okay, I guess.

[Silence]

Eve: It's been… difficult.

[Silence]

Eve: It's been hard, I guess. I just… It's hard. I haven't seen anyone. Not really. My neighbour brought me some food. That was nice. Not the food, but her bringing me it. The food wasn't nice. Oh, I feel bad now. I shouldn't have said that. I hadn't seen anyone in days. She knocked on my door and I got excited to see someone… anyone. But then I was so scared. My heart started beating fast. I opened the door and she smiled and said hello. But I panicked. I just stared at her. Oh, I feel terrible thinking about it. She handed me the food and said something, I can't even remember what she said, isn't that bad? I took it and shut the door without a word. God, what is wrong with me? What is wrong with me? Someone does something nice and I can't even show any appreciation. I panic like a child. I am a child. Aren't I?

I know you think I am, everybody does. Don't you? Oh, don't answer that.

[Silence]

And that was it. For the rest of the week it's been all I can think of. How sweet my neighbour is, how caring and kind. And how horrible I am. This anxiety. This bloody anxiety, it makes me horrible. Oh, I shouldn't have sworn. I am sorry. But it makes me rude. To everyone. Everyone terrifies me, and I can't say anything I want to say. All this week I've been thinking about how I could have talked to my neighbour. I don't even know her name, aren't I horrible. It's just been going around and around and around in my head. How I should have acted, what I should have said. In my head, I talk to her, I say thank you, I ask her her name… I am just a normal person. But I'm not a normal person, am I? I have a normal person, somewhere in my head, who isn't terrified of everything. But I am not normal. I'm miles away from normal. Little Miss Terrified. That'd be my Little Miss character. Little Miss Terrified. Although, no children would want to read about me. It would probably depress them to death. Then they'd end up like me.

[Silence]

So that's my week. My terrible week, to add to a long line of terrible weeks. You only asked me one question and I haven't shut up. I am sorry. I must be a useless patient. Do you dread seeing me? I bet you do… don't you? Oh, please don't answer that. 'Oh, here she comes, little miss terrified, the longest hour of my day', is that what you think? If it's not, then you must be mad! Oh, please don't answer that.

Dr C: Eve, I have told you before, but will tell you again: I look forward to our time together. I care about you and respect you. I do not think you are a child, but I do think you feel like a child a lot of the time.

You said that this anxiety makes you horrible, and I've noticed you've said that before. I'm wondering if we could explore that a little.

Eve: Okay. Oh, that was nice... what you said.

Dr C: I meant it.

Eve: Well, it is like I said, it makes me into a horrible person. I get anxious in all social situations. Even... I mean... just now, with the receptionist, she smiled at me and said something nice, and I panicked and just turned away and sat down. It's like, I'm so scared of talking. It's like... I suppose... I'm always worried what people will think of me. If I go to talk it might come out wrong. I might say something stupid. I'm not good at that kind of thing. And so, I just say nothing.

Dr C: So, you are scared of how people will judge you, and yet, it seems by saying nothing at all you come across, in your words, as "horrible".

Eve: Yeah. Exactly. Oh... yeah that is right. I am afraid of what they'll think of me, so I don't say anything. I don't even look them in the eye. But, as a result, they probably think that I'm rude. They probably think that I am a rude person. Maybe, I am a rude person. And yet, there is always a part of me, that knows what to say. That is telling me, "say hello for god sake!" or "say thank you and smile for god sake!" There is a part of me that knows how to act, but it gets overridden by my anxiety. Like my anxiety is too big, it blocks the normal person out.

Dr C: Tell me more about this other part of you.

Eve: Oh, okay. I think of her as me, but without anxiety. She is just how I want to be. She is confident, smart. I…

[Silence]

Dr C: go on…

Eve: This is a little embarrassing… but… she is also quite… umm… flirtatious. She tells me what I should say, she flirts with men she thinks are attractive.

Dr C: You refer to this other part of yourself as "she", as if it is a separate person to yourself.

Eve: That is how it feels. She is so different to me. She is the opposite of me. She is everything I want to be. It is so frustrating, I know she is in there, but my fear… my bloody anxiety is preventing her from taking control. Oh, I swore again, I am sorry.

Dr C: You don't need to apologise for swearing Eve, it is perfectly acceptable here. I noticed you smiling when talking about "her".

Eve: Sometimes I imagine that she is in the driving seat. It makes me happy, relaxed, excited. I get a tingly feeling all over when I imagine myself confident, strong, sexy. Oh my god, I just said sexy. I am sorry. But she is. She wouldn't care what people thought of her. She would just be free. Free to say how she feels, act how she wants, do what makes her happy. You're right, I can feel myself smile as I talk about it. It feels like I am free, for a moment, when I talk about her, I am free from my anxiety. Or, at least, I am imagining I am free. Like I've been walled in all this time. A ring of wall surrounding me. No windows, no door, just brick after brick all around and as far up as you can see. And not just one layer, but… maybe… twenty layers. Yes. Twenty layers of brick wall locking me in from the outside world. That part of me that is normal can see the world, can say what she wants to say, but the bricks block her out from having any control over this body. Just the anxiety… the fear has control. Controls everything. The way I feel, what I do, and don't do, what I say. She is in there, somewhere, like a princess locked in a castle.

Dr C: I'm wondering, who is in control in this room? Is it your anxiety, "her", or someone else?

Eve: Oh… um…

[Silence]

Eve: I guess. It's not her. It's not her. I know, because she is still telling me what to say and I'm ignoring it. But I don't act like I do with other people. I can talk. I am not afraid of what you think of me. Well, that is not true. I am. I also wonder what you think of me. I guess it is just safer in here. So, it is somewhere in between her and my anxiety. Out there, in the real world, it is my anxiety. In here, it is something in between. I don't know… I don't know…

Dr C: And Eve, what would it feel like, to break down some of those walls?

Eve: Oh… I do think about that. It is kind of a combination between terrified and excited.

Dr C: Terrified and excited.

Eve: Yeah. Like, terrified because… she'll be free. There will be nothing holding her back. It's like, she is contained and a prisoner, but that is at least safe. But, if she becomes free, there's no getting her back. She'll be out there, in the world. Talking to people, doing things I wouldn't dream of. Maybe, she has been boxed up for so long that she'll go wild. I feel like, if she were let out, I'd be in the passenger seat, just watching whatever she does without any control. Or maybe, I'd replace her, behind the wall. And there'll still be one part of me outside the wall and one part of me inside. Oh… yeah. That is quite scary.

Dr C: You also mentioned excited.

Eve: Excited. Well, the things that scare me also excite me. Imagine being the opposite of myself right now. Imagine that confidence, that freeness. Imagine not caring. Just not caring at all. Imagine putting my anxiety behind that wall. Just a distant voice with no power over me. It just feels…

[Silence]

Dr C: It feels…

Eve: Oh, terrible. Hopeless. Talking about it now. I imagined it and it made me happy for a while. But I know that it won't happen. That it can't happen. She's too far gone; I am too weak. The wall is too deep, too high. Oh, look at me now, crying. I am sorry. I bet you can't stand me crying in front of you. You know we have never had a session where I haven't cried. Not one. It's pathetic. I'm pathetic. Oh, what must you think of me?

Dr C: Eve, I'm interested in who has built this wall.

Chapter 5 – The Tracks

There he was again, on the train tracks. He looked up. He looked behind and side to side. Nothing but darkness. Black, all around, except the tracks under his feat, and as far as he could see in front and behind. He noticed his feet, both on one rotten wooden plank, one of thousands making up the tracks. Kept in place by two steel brackets connected to two unending lines of cold, thick steel. It was cold. He could suddenly feel the coldness chill his bare forearms. It crept upwards and settled in at the back of his upper arms, drawing out the goosebumps and making him shudder.

The tracks started to vibrate, ever so slightly. He could feel it in his toes and deep inside his head. Something was coming. Something big. Ahead seemed the obvious option. In fact, looking back became hard. He turned his neck, but his feet wouldn't move, and his hips were stuck aiming forward. He could feel his spine struggle to twist, like a set of rusted bearings he could feel it grind slowly around until he could see behind. Then pain. Sharp pain, in the centre of his head, just where he could sense the vibration. He winced his eyes as the pain blurred his vision and slowly crawled down his spine, vertebrae by vertebrae. It burnt now. He gave in and spun his head back to face forward like releasing a spring. The pain vanished, and the chill on his arms returned to consciousness. Forward was definitely the way.

He followed the tracks, step-by-step, one rotten piece of wood at a time. He could feel them crumble under his feet. Each step providing a damp crack of wood, uselessly trying to keep its shape under his weight. As he progressed the tracks got worse. There were only hints of wood where some pieces used to be. Bare splinters and mould. The steel became warped, bending outwards and losing its grip on the wood. It lost its shine, its coldness, and instead became rusted, cracked, an array of harsh browns and greys. The kind that gets stuck under your nails or splinters into your skin, only to stay there for days, a constant reminder.

The vibrations increased. He wriggled his numb toes to bring back some feeling. Yes, the vibrations had increased. They brought with them a sense of panic. His arms were getting colder, his body uselessly attempting to shiver his goosebumps away. He rubbed the back of his arms with his hands. The thin whiteness of warm breath on cold air was visible with each exhalation, but only for a second, before floating away into the darkness. The panic. Something was coming. His heart beats dragged themselves closer together, preparing for something, he could sense their nervousness. The hairs on the back of his neck pricked up, they too knew something was coming. His speed increased. Now he could hear the crunch of each bit of old track under his feet.

Small stones sprang to life, lifting themselves off the floor a centimetre as the whole earth shook. A centimetre, then an inch, then two inches. He struggled to place his feet now on the unsteady ground. Trying with all his will to aim his feet in the desired place, just for that place to be wrenched away at the last second. He was running now, but almost falling over every few steps. He missed the track, clipping the corroded steel with the outside of his left foot. The sharp, piercing pain. His ankle twisted inwards. Pain rushed in all directions, up his shin, down to his toes, like a knife carved up through his bone. It brought warmth, a silver lining, he could feel his toes once again. But no time to stop. He limped on, gritting his teeth and squinting his eyes with each brief, pathetic step on his left foot.

He saw them first by a faint glow illuminating the tracks ahead. As if someone was holding up a lit candle, he could see a dim light presenting the upcoming tracks. It grew, as if the sun was slowly rising behind him, the tracks became ever slightly clearer. But, unlike the sunrise, this light wasn't welcome. He didn't know it's source, but he could sense its purpose and it brought fear, as well as near hopelessness, to consume his thoughts. He slowed now, not due to the unbearable pain shooting up from his ankle, nor due to the unknown source of the intensifying light, but due to what, with the aid of the light, he could now see in front of him. Although he couldn't see it as such, it wasn't something that could be seen, more a void of sight. A place where vision stopped. About thirty metres in front of him, clear as day although darker than night, it consumed. It ate the tracks and the light, all things ceased at its beginning, an infinite wall of blackness. Black like he'd never seen before, not like black paint, or the night sky or when you close your eyes, in fact it wasn't black at all, but simply a lack of anything, a pure and silent nothingness. He stared in terrified awe. The end of the tracks. His eyes were fixed, unable to look away but so desperate to at the same time.

The silence was broken. *Chuka-chuka chuka-chuka chuka-chuka chuka-chuka.* The sound was deafening and close behind him. He knew what it was now, and he was right to be afraid. The vibrations increased, the lights were blinding, and the sound filled his skull. He tried to turn his head to get a glimpse, but it was impossible. His neck was cemented in place and his eyes transfixed, hypnotised it seemed, on what was ahead.

He had nowhere to go but forward, as the sound galloped its way towards him. He limped forward, carefully, slowly. He knew his only two options, he would do anything to have a third. *Chuka-chuka chuka-*

chuka chuka-chuka chuka-chuka. Fifteen-metres away, he picked up his pace. *Chuka-chuka chuka-chuka.* Ten-metres away. He was breathing heavily but the sound of his breath was immediately pounced on by what was approaching. *Chuka-chuka chuka-chuka.* Then he was there, the end of the tracks. Face-to-face with the nothingness, the consumer of all things. He felt its power, its presence loomed over him, he was tiny, pathetic, an unnoticeable dot before the great wall. He brought his right hand up and moved it to within a centimetre of the wall, it felt nothing. He only had seconds left now before the provider of the sound and light ran through him like a sledgehammer hitting a pin. Deep breath, and he pushed his right hand forward, into the darkness, beyond sight. He lost his breath. He tried to scream but it was trapped at the base of his throat. The ice formed as he quickly lost all movement of each digit, frozen into place. Without thought his left hand dragged his right back into sight. He tried to look at it, to comprehend its frozen state. But it was too late. The noise had caught up with him. The lights had caught up with him. In a feeble attempt, he braced himself…

Chapter 6 – Day Dreamer

'Today we bury Brennan. Husband to an unfulfilled wife, son to unimpressed parents, brother to a superior being. Dull was his life, nothing noteworthy to mention, to be honest. Seventy years of sleepwalking and daydreaming, in a nutshell. It'll probably only take a few years before Brennan no longer even exists in mere memories and passing thoughts…'

'Brennan!'

All the faces around the table were aimed at him now. *Oh god*, he thought, *he had drifted away again.*

'Are you with us now, Brennan?' said with a look that oozed disdain. One his boss' face naturally made when considering Brennan; something he tried to do as little as possible.

'Sorry, boss,' Brennan managed, whilst red filled his pudgy cheeks. The faces lingered at him for a second more before turning away again. He sneaked a glance at his watch. Ninety whole bloody minutes left. He hated meetings. He hated nearly everything about work, but at the top of his hateful hierarchy was meetings. It felt like a weekly punishment, never was he consulted, asked a question, even looked at unless he was being harshly reminded that naps were not permitted. No information had Brennan ever taken from a meeting that benefitted his role as the company accountant. Admittedly, actually listening to the content or reading the minutes may have provided something tenable to use, but it just bored him to death. He remembered what his mum used to say, 'only boring people get bored.' He hated that saying. And she was probably right. He was confident he was as boring as they came. Probably the reason why no one at work ever said more than "good morning" or "see you tomorrow" to him. He didn't invite conversation, the idea of small talk seemed so forced and dull he could only do it ironically. There was just nothing to discuss, he had no interests except his embarrassing collection of rare coins, and he wasn't about to raise this in conversation anytime soon. He didn't enjoy football, he had no real hobbies, he didn't have any children, he was sure his wife only stayed with him out of pity. In fact, he was sure that no one talked to him because he would certainly bore them to death. Even his face gave away his complete lack of substance. If people found out he was a robot they would probably say, 'you know that makes a lot of sense.'

There were more interesting days, not too long ago. There were friends and they would go for a beer once a week to the local. The highlight of Brennan's week.

They would all moan about their jobs, their wives, their new aches and pains, aging. It kept him sane, but he only realised this after it was too late. One of them died from cancer, the others either moved away for work or drifted away. He was certainly not going to embarrass himself by contacting them first, but he wished for those beer filled Friday evenings to return. Although, in truth, he was concerned about what they'd all make of him now. Everyone had moved on, moved up in the world, better jobs, better houses, children. He was exactly the same, not a thing had changed. He feared their pity.

'Brennan!'

Oh god, he'd done it again.

'Anything to add?' his boss asked, praying for Brennan to say something worthy of immediate dismissal and sacking from the company. A slight smile crept at the corner of his lips as he imagined never having to lay eyes on his accountant again, on his scruffy untouched curly hair or his creased white shirt two sizes too big for him.

If I hurled myself out of this window, would the fall be enough to end my life or just badly injure me, Brennan thought. 'No, boss. Nothing to add,' he said rather chirpily, dreaming of the fall to the concrete outside.

His old Mondeo took him home, through the murky, gentle rain. The kind that doesn't fall but sits in the air waiting to be driven into. Before arriving, he picked up a bottle of wine for Amora from the corner shop. He first did this in an attempt to be romantic, spontaneous even, but, like everything else in their marriage, it had now just become routine. He'd get home, 'Hi Bren,' Amora would greet him, one of only a handful of people ever to call him Bren. They'd kiss, just a peck on the lips, handing her the wine she would say thank you. Then she'd open it, hand him a beer out the fridge and ask about his day. And he'd tell her, not that he wanted to, it was just what they did. His wife would listen politely, usually responding with, 'your boss is a bit of a dick you know.'

Brennan would often defend him, 'oh he's okay.' Why on earth did he defend him, he often wondered. He *was* a bit of a dick. His boss was the worst. *I probably deserve him*; he'd mope to himself. She'd make dinner, they'd watch an episode or two of their current series, then they'd go to bed with another peck on the lips to seal the day.

Except, of course, on Thursdays. Due to a long drought, Amora proposed Thursdays as their sex night. Only one episode with dinner to ensure they are not too tired. Then ten minutes of sex, preceded by a well routinised order of foreplay. Even sex had become routinised. He knew he was to blame, always being too tired, too stressed or just not up for it. The truth was that he struggled to get it up and was still too young for this to be deemed acceptable. He refused to talk about it, and even though he knew his wife knew, they both humoured the ignorance. He was grateful for that, and for the effort she put in to getting it up most nights. However, it often took his ugly imagination of some unsightly sexual scenes, scenarios that would haunt another's nightmares, in order to become erect. A slightly younger, reasonably good-looking colleague once touched him on the arm whilst talking to him and giggled. He was sure he wasn't funny, but likewise was sure no one would flirt with him. Now that poor girl was often the counterpart in these fantasies to help him perform. Perform, being an overstatement of course, there were no awards being won in that bedroom. But it was enough for them to maintain a facade that their marriage was okay.

It wasn't okay, however. Gone was any hint of a spark, of joy, of spontaneity in their marriage. Brennan knew this and knew he was to blame. However, he resented his wife for it. Not for the lack, so much as her response. It all seemed ironic. Her polite smile when asking him about his day, kissing him on the lips, telling him she loved him, ringing him at work and, surely, faking orgasms on a Thursday. He knew, she dreamed of someone else. Some hunk, with thicker hair, features which didn't resemble playdough, an interesting job, interesting stories, someone who would randomly take her away to Paris or some other horribly romantic destination. He knew that she thought of this man, perfectly formed over years of sculpting in her imagination, whenever she saw him. That's why she could seem so happy, so smiley, throughout this whole joke of a marriage. He hated that man. He imagined him swooping in and taking his wife away from him, finally freeing her from this prison. Mostly, however, he hated his wife for inventing him.

He parked up in his drive as a Subaru growled past and down their cul-de-sac. The local boy racers. The amount of money spent on that disgusting car, he thought. Spoilers, lowered, an exhaust you could fit a football up. His first thought was of jumping out in front of the car as it sped past. If he was lucky enough it would kill him. In fact, he pondered, if he timed it right he could not only kill himself, he could ruin their lives also by making it look like they ran him over. Perhaps hiding behind the bushes and then diving out onto a zebra crossing when they approached. Their street would be greatly improved that day. He sighed.

Leaving the car, he got to the front door and noticed his neighbour on their drive, looking up to the evening sky. *What an oddball*, he mused. Looking around, he noticed half the street out. Joining he craned his neck to the sky. Small white dots crossed the sky, thirty or forty planes, or so it seemed, all clustered together, a million miles away. He had remembered something on the news about a meteor shower, come to think of it. He watched them pass overhead. Opening the front door, Amora gave him a kiss and a big smile. 'How pretty.' She awed whilst watching the show in the sky. Bren gave a paper-thin smile, a shallow mask of the emotions behind it.

'Hi, sweetheart,' he managed. *Patronising bitch*, he thought.

Chapter 7 – The Wall

Eve: You know I've thought a lot about that question you asked me last week, 'who has built the wall?' blocking in Evie. Oh, yeah, I gave her a name by the way, it's Evie. She's me, but more… so Evie. If you think about it, it's thirty percent more. So, it's kind of like thirty percent of me is trapped away. Oh, ummm, what was I saying?

Dr C: You said you have thought a lot about who built the wall.

Eve: Oh, yes, thank you. Well, I have. All week in fact, every day it's been on my mind: who built the wall? And I thought of all the things that have happened to me that have made me this way. You know a lot of it, Dr C, what I've been through. I bet there are enough bad experiences in my life to have a brick per each in that giant wall. And so, well, I didn't know where to start, but I wanted to work out the answer, I've been obsessed with it. I feel, if I know how that wall was built, I'll know how to take it down. So, I've written it down. I've filled this whole diary look. It probably doesn't make any sense to other people, it's a bit of a mess... it's a lot of a mess, but I can understand it. Would you like to see?

Dr C: Why don't you pick a page or a few and talk me through them?

Eve: Oh, okay. That's probably better. I don't know if you'd be able to make any sense of it. Oh, not saying you're stupid. You're obviously very intelligent. Oh, I meant... just...

Dr C: Eve, it is okay. I never thought you were insinuating I was stupid. Why don't you describe a page to me?

Eve: Oh, okay... good. Right, a page. So, I'll just skip to one then. Here we go. I was eight and in my bedroom drawing. I could hear screaming downstairs. I was used to arguments and hid away in my bedroom most of the time. But this sounded different. I could hear my mum in pain. I wanted to go and protect her, but I was very scared. I crept down the stairs and whispered loudly, 'Mum... mum?' But she didn't answer. She was no longer screaming but crying loudly. I went to the bottom of the stairs and followed the sound; it was coming from the kitchen. I needed to protect my mum, so I was brave and opened the door. I didn't scream, but just stared at the blood on the floor. I couldn't make sense of it. My mum was in the corner of the kitchen, curled up on the floor, she was holding the side of her face and blood was coming out of her nose. She had blood down her top and her pyjama bottoms.

She was mumbling, I think it was "leave us alone, leave us alone" over and over again. I looked up and saw my dad, standing over the kitchen sink with his arm under the tap. The water from the tap was hitting his wrist and flowing red with blood off his elbow into the sink. He had a big gash straight down his forearm, it must've been about five inches long.

He was mumbling too. 'Fucking psycho bitch,' I heard him say. Then there was a kitchen knife on the floor, also with blood all over it. Like I said I stared, I was so shocked. I saw all the blood and I panicked, I felt dizzy, then I was sick, all over the floor. I had been standing there for ten seconds at least, but my mum didn't notice me until I was sick. She crawled over to me and put her hand on my face.

'Don't look, honey' she said. I noticed her other hand was planted in my sick, she didn't even realise. My dad didn't seem to notice I was there. I ran up to my bedroom, closed the door and sat leaning on the inside of it so they couldn't get in. But they didn't even try. I didn't hear much else that day. Mum told me food was ready in the evening, but I didn't leave my room. The next day I came out and my dad was gone. My mum had a big bruise on her eye, her cheek and lip were swollen on the same side, her nose was a bit crooked. I asked her where Dad was, but she just ignored the question. That was the last I saw of him for two years. My mum just pretended nothing happened.

[Silence]

Eve: So… that is this page. You know I think that is also why I am so fearful of being sick. It terrifies me. I can never eat very much because I am afraid of throwing it up, it's why I am so skinny. That image, my mother's hand in my sick, it makes me shudder with fear. But I think I worked that out… isn't that great?

Dr C: You've never told me that story in so much detail, and yet this is the first time you've told it without crying.

Eve: I know. But, it's kind of… it makes sense to me now, for the first time. Before, it was traumatic, senseless, it was painful. But now, it explains who I am… or why I am like this.

Dr C: It is a part of the wall?

Eve: Yes. Exactly. But only a small part. Like I said only one brick, or maybe a breeze block, but there are so many of these.

Dr C: Would you be willing to share anymore?

Eve: Yes, I want to share them all with you. There are loads you haven't heard, and I finally feel like I can share with you. Let's see… Oh, yes, how about this one:

I was thirteen. There was a boy at school who bullied me, a lot. It started with him always barging past me in the corridors. He made a point of knocking me with his shoulder. I just ignored it; I was scared of him to be honest. Then he started to laugh at me in class. When teachers used to ask me questions, I became so nervous

I would just clam up, my face would go red, it felt like everyone was staring at me. Some teachers learnt to not ask me, but others were so persistent they made me cry. Anyway, in one of these classes he would laugh whenever I was asked a question and he would shout "speak up!" to me all the time. Actually, that was his nickname for me. He would shout it at me whenever he saw me. 'Speak up, Eve! We can't hear you.' It used to make others laugh. It made me cry a lot. Eventually, I went to tell one of the nicer teachers who didn't ask me questions. I told him what was happening. I cried and he held my hand and said he would deal with it. It made me feel so relieved. The next day at school he took me out of class and said he'd like to see me every morning to check in with me. It made me excited, someone to talk to, someone who was looking out for me. So, the next day I went straight to his classroom. He locked the door, for privacy, he said. Then he held my hand and stroked it as he asked me questions, when I cried about the bullying, he wiped the tears of my face. It made me feel cared for, no one ever held my hand, not even my own mother, I thought he was just being nice. But it got worse, gradually. He started putting his hand on my leg. He told me to take my jumper and tie off and undo some buttons. He said it would help me relax. God, I was so stupid, so naive. I did it. The next day he'd ask for more buttons. One day he had his hand right at the top of my leg and was squeezing it.

I asked him to move his hand because it was hurting and he told me, 'I am just trying to help, you need to trust me, okay?' He didn't move it. That's when I started to get scared. I stopped wanting to go to school. I faked being ill and my mum kept me off school, but after a week she forced me to go back. I pleaded with her, but she wouldn't listen. I didn't want to tell her what was happening, I felt so stupid. I was afraid she wouldn't believe me. After the week off he wasn't nice anymore, he was demanding and mean. I used to run into school and hide in the toilets. I was terrified of what he'd do to me, if he knew I'd been hiding. I decided I needed to get kicked out of school, that was the only way I'd be free from him. So, one day, I stole a knife from my kitchen, put it in my bag and walked into school. I didn't know what I was going to do with it. No one had found out and it was the last lesson of the day. So, while miss was talking, I took out the knife and just held it on the desk. The girl next to me screamed and jumped away from me. Miss told me to hand it over, I asked her will she kick me out of school, and she said if you hand it over maybe not. I couldn't take that risk, so I held it up, I didn't know what I was going to do, I just knew this was the time, I had to do something. The boy next to me tried to move out of the way, it scared me, I swung the knife and caught him in the palm of the hand. The rest was a blur. I dropped the knife, got walked to the head's office, my mum picked me up and I was taken home. The boy, apparently, wasn't too badly hurt and the parents said they wouldn't press charges if I was excluded. I never returned to the school. At the time I couldn't have been happier. It was a success, I was free, free of him. I never considered that I wouldn't be allowed into any other normal school. But, my other schooling, that's on many other pages.

Dr C: Eve, you are right, I have never heard that story before. It sounded so frightening, and yet, again, you told it with so little emotion.

Eve: I know, I was always too afraid to go back over it. Like… going back over it would make me relive the experience. I didn't want to go through that again. But now, like with the story about my dad, it makes sense. It explains me. It explains how Evie has been locked away. It is another brick, another part of that wall. Would you like to hear another one? There are so many you don't know about that I can finally share.

Dr C: Well, Eve, I would very much like to hear more. However, we are coming towards the end of our time. It's been a very enlightening session and you seem in a better place than last week. You started the session with the question, 'who has built the wall?' So, I'm wondering, what have you learnt about the answer?

Eve: Well…

[Silence]

All those experiences built the wall. But who? Well, I guess… it's like each one of them brought a brick and placed it down, cemented it in place. My dad cemented a brick, my mum cemented a brick, the bullies, that teacher, my old roommates, my doctor… they all walked up inside my head and cemented down a brick, to lock away a part of my soul. A part of me.

[Silence]

Oh, here I go again. You can see that made me upset. I nearly went a whole session without crying.

Dr C: Cemented in place. Can you knock them down?

Eve: Only with a sledgehammer.

Chapter 8 – Superior Intellect

'Oh yes, come in, come in,' he said, with an ironic, almost mocking, smile. 'Sit down on the sofa here, let me get you some coffee.'

The guests sat awkwardly on the sofa, their buttocks half over the edge, not daring to make themselves at home. So unusual was their invite into a home, they were hardly prepared for such an occurrence. Their host, too, seemed odd and this put them on edge, with his peculiar smile as he ushered them in. Neither of them wanted to admit they felt it, but they both thought he might be making a joke out of them, or was simply strange, or worse, some sort of murderer. Both of them males, slight and in smart navy suit trousers, brown shoes and clean white shirts with navy ties, sat in anticipation.

'Here, coffees and milk, I assume you don't take sugar? Must be a sin right, ha!' Bren smiled to himself. 'So, you are here to talk to me about God?' Bren smiled at them both. It was a kind smile, but he couldn't quite hide the excited malice behind it. In his head, Bren was putting out a raw bit of meat and enticing these puppies towards it, only to catch them in his cage, and he was struggling to contain his excitement at it all.

'Yes, and Jesus,' one of the men responded.

'Excellent. How rude of me, what are your names?' Bren responded, acting as courteously as he could muster, though its thinness was quite apparent to any observer. He learnt they were called Theo and Gabe. 'Well, please, go ahead.'

Both men seemed hoping the other would jump in first. Theo eventually responded. 'Well, we wanted to talk to you about the love of God and... and why you should let God into your life. Are you religious, sir?'

"Why should I let God into my life?" Bren inquired, deliberately avoiding the question, he wanted to keep them guessing a while before he unleashed his intelligence upon them.

'Yes, you see,' responded Gabe, seeming a little more confident, 'God is the light and the way, and he showed us the way through Jesus. Are you familiar with the stories of Jesus? You see, Jesus was the human embodiment of the Lord. He came down to show us, the people, how we can follow the way of the Lord. Jesus did this through showing unconditional love to all humanity. He taught us to even love our enemies and to want the best for them. But Jesus knew that man was not able to fulfil his example, unlike him they were destined to sin. So, Jesus made the greatest act of selflessness, he died *for* our sins. He died so that we may be forgiven for not being able to live as he did on earth. Instead, God will accept our noble efforts to try our very best to live as Jesus did.' Gabe was getting himself quite excited now and felt on a roll, he spoke passionately and clearly, quite proud of his efforts. 'So, we must, sir, attempt to live as Jesus did. We must show kindness to our fellow man, we must pray to God the Father and have faith in his decisions, no matter how confusing they may be to us, they all make sense to God, but we do not have the ability to *understand* much of his plan. This is why on the cross Jesus shouts out, "My God, why hast thou forsaken me?" Do you see? Jesus was in human form. The human is unable to comprehend the motives of God, it is the human form that does not allow it. So, we must have faith that all of God's actions are in our good, no matter how odd they may seem to us.'

Bren was nodding along, enthusiastically, as an adult may nod along to a child's tale. 'And all happenings on Earth are God's actions?' he inquired.

'Yes,' said Gabe. 'All are God's actions. Every one of them. All that seems good, great and bad, are the actions of God.' He was positively ecstatic now, discussing this, the topic he knew more about than any other. Theo nodded along enthusiastically, impressed by his friend's clarity and confidence.

'So.' Bren was ready to pounce. 'The abolition of slavery, the end of the holocaust, democracy, all actions of God?

'Yes, exactly... yes,' they both agreed, eagerly. Nodding their heads in excitement.

'And so, slavery itself, the holocaust and tyrannical government must all have been actions of God too, in that perspective?' Bren asked, as if he had only just thought of this argument then and there.

The guests' excitement quickly soured, and they became awkward and fidgety. 'Well...' Gabe said, tentatively, as if he knew what the response would be. 'God works in mysterious ways, we cannot understand his plan.'

A pitying smile appeared on Bren's lips, he was all too prepared for this and he found it a shame these boys weren't better prepared to challenge him. 'I can appreciate that perhaps God is superior and thus to comprehend his plan is impossible to us mere humans. But, surely... *surely,* the fact that his plan contains the brutal murder, torture, starvation, castration, beheading and so on, of innocent people who pray to him, causes you some concern? Some trepidation that, perhaps, this God is somewhat malevolent? That he enjoys violence and suffering? That he views humans as pawns, as playthings, and not as beings worthy of his unconditional love? The way I see it, gentlemen, is that if God is all powerful and yet there is so much suffering, unnecessary suffering, that maybe he is simply not that nice? Why, in this case, must we assume that he is so benevolent?' Bren raised his eyebrows with this question, attempting to act as if he was engaged in a mutual conversation with them. How he really felt, however, was that these two men were, quite frankly, brainwashed idiots who didn't know how to think for themselves at all and, as a result, he was in a position to crush them with his intelligence and enjoy every minute of doing so.

Theo and Gabe looked awkwardly at the floor, neither wanting to make eye contact with him. Both, now, wanting to leave this house with their tail between their legs, rather than continue down this path, of which they did not believe would end well.

'There is,' Theo eventually said, with a childish triumph, 'free will. Yes, humans do have free will and, therefore, their actions are their own. When Eve ate the apple from the Tree of The Knowledge of Good and Evil, the "scales fell from her eyes". She became a conscious being, aware of her past and future. Her and Adam were kicked out of the Garden of Eden and made to work. Ever since, they have had free will, able to decide on their decisions. As we mentioned, humans are inevitably sinful, therefore, in our free will some humans will sin, some a great deal. But others will follow in Jesus' footsteps and put things right. That's why slavery started, and slavery ended. It was because of humans, *not* because of God.' Theo was quite proud of himself and was able to bring himself, during the speech, to hold eye contact with Brennan. The latter listened, appearing attentive, already knowing the argument that was being put forward.

Brennan left a silence before responding, playing with his prey. 'So, God gave us free will?'

'Yes.' Theo nodded.

'And God is all powerful, all knowing?'

'Yes.' Another pleased nod from Theo.

'Then, in giving us free will, God must have predicted that, in doing so, he would cause slavery, the holocaust, torture etc. He must have seen this, or he is not all knowing.' Bren couldn't hold back anymore.

'The way I see it, boys,' he started, superciliously, 'is there are only two options here, both of which you have outlined yourselves. Either, God is all powerful and in control of everything, *or* God gave us free will. In the first instance, God is directly responsible for all the terrible atrocities on Earth and, no matter what his inaccessible plan is, that is a fact and a crime beyond comprehension. If it is the latter, God either knew that by giving us free will, he will cause all of the atrocities to follow, therefore he acted in a way to allow them to happen, or he didn't know they were going to happen, in which case he is not all-knowing. If he is not all-knowing, then maybe he really isn't worth praying to, if you ask me. There is another option though, consider this. There is... no God. The Earth was created by chance due to the laws of science, the Bible is a fantastic book of stories, but that is all. Religion has no place in our society, it has caused war and death and remains in place now, purely to keep the powerful, powerful. You go to church every week, along with all the old fools who go too, they give their pound to the collection, thinking they are contributing to a kind priest. This money adds up and gets funnelled to fund those high priests, and the pope, with no benefit to humankind. Religion is, simply, duping people out of their money for the powerful. And you people, you brainwashed people unable to think for yourselves, think you are doing good. When in fact, you are supporting an evil, a relic from the past. I know it all, I know all the arguments for religion and none of them make sense to me. There is just one thing about religion I can't get my head around...' A sly smile grew on Brennan's face as he looked at both boys in turn in the eyes. '...why are so many priests paedophiles? Maybe you could answer that for me?'

Both were clearly shocked by this rant, but the last question left their mouths open with disbelief. With an attempted sternness, yet a noticeable shakiness either from anger or anxiety Bren couldn't tell, Gabe managed after a silence, 'I can see we are not going to influence you on the topic today. We shall leave you in peace. Thank you for the coffee.'

Upon leaving, Gabe turned around a few steps down the front path and said to Brennan the first unanticipated thing he had heard from either of them. With a kind soft voice, he said, 'You know, you are obviously intelligent and think a great deal. We will not beat you at a battle of intellect. However, I have seen many times men with great intelligence and no concept of the transcendent suffer greatly. They suffer more than the unintelligent and more than the religious. I am afraid you have a similar fate.' With that the two left.

Bren was originally ecstatic about how he had torn the two boys apart, how he had dominated them so easily. *All religious types are the same*, he thought. But with this last comment from Gabe he was quite frustrated. Firstly, he didn't get the last word in, how infuriating that was. But also, the thought of such an idiot pitying him, worrying for him as if *he*, Brennan, were the one to be pitied in this whole situation. It was unbearably frustrating. He took the coffee and mugs back into the kitchen. Staring at the mugs for some time, lost in thought, his mind went away. Then his usual sadness came over him. He told himself it stemmed from *those* people being the norm. How dumb most people were, how depressed it made him with the world. If only there were some more intelligent people about, the world would be a more bearable place to live. The truth was, however, that that conversation was the most socialising he had had for a very long time. Now, they were gone, never to return. The cause of his sadness now was a deep loneliness and isolation. Although, he wouldn't dare entertain this possible cause, yet alone admit to it.

Chapter 9 – Dreams

Joel's entire body flinched a centimetre off the mattress. He could feel his heart attempting to leave his ribcage. His head was damp, and his pillow soaked with sweat. The room was a blur due to eyes that weren't fully awake yet. The pain. He reached a hand down to his left ankle. Relief. It didn't hurt to touch, but the pain lingered from the dream for a few more seconds, ensuring he wouldn't forget that fearful state. Deep breathe in, deep breathe out. His heartbeat calming, Joel rubbed his eyes clear, sat up at the side of the bed and checked his clock. 3 a.m. Always 3 a.m. But this one was worse than previous ones. Not the content, that was the same, but the emotion, the feeling of the dream, it was more intense, more real. Checking over his shoulder, Rayna was still sleeping, he quietly opened his journal and logged the dream in the same detailed manner as always.

He'd learnt well that attempting sleep now was futile. Checking in on his daughter, sleeping, blissfully free from his personal night-time torments, thank god. He would sacrifice all his sleeping hours to save her from such fear. He made his way, quietly, downstairs. Usually, the silver lining of waking at this time would be the absolute peace, the complete void of noise, for him to read. He thought, however, as he boiled the kettle and prepared his French press coffee, he was too disturbed by the dream this particular morning to appreciate it. He could still feel the slight tremble in his legs as he made his way to the armchair.

The problem was that Joel believed in the importance of dreams. He had, for a long time, written them down when he could remember them and attempted to decode their meaning. Many times it had served him well. He thought of the dream he had during a period his studies and work travel took him far from his family for too long:

He was staring at his family, his wife and daughter. He noticed sand underneath his feat. He went to walk towards them, but he was unable to move his legs. As panic set it the sand began to slowly give way, it was sucking him up. As he sank a wind picked up and took his wife and daughter away, one limb at a time. He watched as their arms flew off, then their legs, then their torsos and finally their heads.

Or the time shortly after both his parents died within the same week:

Two giant snakes had wrapped their long bodies from his feet to his chest, squeezing his arms against his body. He couldn't move. They slowly raised their heads and presented their fangs. They were preparing to devour him, and he was helpless.

Joel had responded to these dreams, he ensured he made the time to spend with his family, he sought support with his grief. It worked. The dreams indicated to him the problems he didn't know he was facing.

Now, however, he had a small glimmer of hope. Hope that maybe, in fact, he was wrong. Hope that dreams didn't actually mean anything, that they were just a random firing of neurons in the brain with no function or purpose, caused by the food you ate that evening or something else arbitrary. False hope, he knew. He let it pass through his thoughts without grasping it. One can't live consciously in untruth, he knew. The alternative, that this brutal nightmare was telling him something. But what? What was approaching him from behind, obviously it must have been a train, but why couldn't he look at it? And what was the blackness, why couldn't he see past it? Why did it freeze his arm? And, why on earth, he wondered, didn't he just step to the side off the tracks?

The coffee soothed his body as he pondered and wrote. Eventually, he moved on, picking up a book to become lost in. The groan of the old cottage pipes gave away his wife's wakeful state. 5 a.m. Early, even for her. He took himself back to the kitchen and prepared her morning coffee. Perhaps she noticed his empty side of the bed and wanted to check on him. He considered whether she'd like pancakes and checked if they had enough flour.

'Have you heard?' A rushed, half-awake mumble.

'Morning. Are you okay? Do you fancy pan…'

'Turn on the news. You need to see this,' Rayna interrupted.

Chapter 10 – Pink Stripe

[Silence]

Dr C: So, do you want to tell me about the hair?

Eve: Oh, I am a little embarrassed about it now. I like it, when I look in the mirror. But when other people see it, I get embarrassed. But it is too late now, I've done it. It was like… after the last session… it was her idea. I've started talking to her, to Evie, I asked her, 'what should I do?' She said I need to set her free. But I don't know how. Neither does she. How can I just let her out? I don't think I have the power to do that. She can't just walk out. She's trapped, and I am powerless. I can talk to her, but it feels useless. I'm still me. I'm still Eve, the scared little girl.

Dr C: So, the hair?

Eve: Oh, yeah, sorry. So, I thought what could I do? How could I bring her out? And it was the only thing I could think of. It is kind of how I picture her hair, bold, confident you know. I was so nervous buying the dye, I felt so stupid, I knew the cashier was thinking how it would never suit me. But I bought it. It took me two days to get the courage to actually do it. But I thought, if I don't do it, I wouldn't have got anywhere. It might not work, but it definitely won't work if I don't actually do it. So, I did. I took this strip of hairs, and put the dye in. It's in my view, I can see it out of my left eye. It makes me think of her. Like a small bit of her has come out.

Dr C: And why pink?

Eve: Well, my hair is brown, boring mousy brown. But bright pink, that's not me, right? That is her. I thought that would represent her best. A little bit of her is free, in my hair, in my view. I am reminded all the time. It's actually helped a little bit. And get this. You will never believe this; I don't even believe it when I think of it. Well, so, I woke up the next morning, and I thought, well now what do I do? Is this it? I'm just me with pink in my hair? I wanted a tea; you know I have a tea first thing every morning. And a wild thought popped into my head, I think she put it there. The thought was that I should go to the cafe and buy a tea from there. Firstly, I was so excited at the idea. But then, oh my god, terrified. I couldn't believe I was even contemplating it. I can't believe it even now. Do you even believe me?

Dr C: I can see by your smile, your excitement and your knees, tucked up to your face, your nervousness.

Eve: Yeah, well. I was nervous. And then… it was like I was a robot. I stopped considering it, stopped thinking about it. I got out of bed, I had a shower, cleaned my teeth, got dressed. You know it usually takes me half the morning to do all those things. But I just did them straight away. Like I said, I was like a robot, like I wasn't in control. I wasn't thinking about anything, just doing. Once I was dressed and ready, I just left my house. Can you believe it? I just left my house. I walked right out, closed the door behind me and headed to the cafe. Then, halfway there, I woke up. I was no longer a robot, it was me, I was actually in the middle of the street walking towards the cafe. My heart started pounding, I noticed people looking at me. I put my head down, stared at my feet. But I thought, *I'll keep going.* I could have turned around, but I didn't. I kept going forward, I couldn't believe I was doing it. But it gets crazier! I got to the cafe, and I walked in. I kept staring at my feet, I felt the whole cafe was staring at me. I walked to the counter and I thought, *well I'm going to have to look up.* And I did. It must have taken me longer than I thought because the man was staring right at me. 'Tea, please?' I said. He smiled and went away to make my tea. My heart was pounding, but I started smiling. I felt so alive! I was terrified and alive. You know I've never done that, never in my life. And then, he returned and asked for money. My hand was shaking getting the money out of my purse, he must have thought I was on drugs. But he gave me my change and I looked right in his eye and I even smiled at him. He smiled back. I looked him in the eyes and smiled. Outside of this room I can't remember the last time I connected with someone like that. He smiled too. I think in that moment I loved him; you know?

Dr C: Can you explain that for me? That feeling of love?

Eve: Oh, umm… no. Not really. I just felt it. Like, I was connected to him. Oh, I feel so silly now, saying this to you. Of course, I don't love him, of course he didn't love me. He just gave me my change. He probably smiled like that at every customer. But at the time it was amazing. I was so proud of myself. I was doing it. But then, oh my god, I couldn't believe it. Then I looked down and he hadn't given me tea. Not a takeaway tea anyway. He gave me a tray, with a pot of tea, a pot of milk and a pot of sugar and a mug. I panicked. It was too much. I thought about what I had to do. I'm starting to sweat now just thinking of it. I had to pick the tray up, walk all the way to a table without dropping anything, place the tray on the table without dropping anything. Then sit down, by myself, surrounded by people staring at me whilst I make the tea. I thought I was going to drop it, or spill my tea trying to make it. I must've been thinking for a while because he asked me if everything was okay. This time I couldn't look at him, I just stared at my feet and walked straight out. I walked straight out and all the way back home. He must have thought I was mad. I am mad, I suppose. I was exhausted then and confused.

Dr C: Confused.

Eve: Yeah, like, what had just happened. It was all so much to take in. I couldn't believe I did it, I still don't now even though I know it is true. Part of me was so happy, proud even, but then I ruined it. It became too much. I made a fool of myself with everyone watching. I didn't know what to make of it all. And then back to worrying about what I did, how people saw me, what I should have done differently. I was stuck in a trance just going over and over and over it. I didn't leave the house, for the rest of the week, until now. I was so tired too. I couldn't turn off; my brain was exhausted. I slept for over twelve hours that night.

Dr C: It sounded like a lot of excitement, of which you are not used to. I want to know, Eve, where were you in all of this? Where was Eve?

Eve: Oh, I don't know. Like… it felt like Evie took me out of the door. She came out and led the way from when I woke up until I was walking to the cafe. Then she kind of lost her grip and I came back on the way there, but I kept on walking which didn't seem like me. Then, in the cafe it was hard to tell… like… it was a bit of me then a bit of her… like we were trying to fuse together, unable to. I don't know, it is all very confusing.

Dr C: And how does it feel now, talking about it?

Eve: Well… it feels like progress, actually. It's exciting and scary. I let her out… or she got out. It's positive. I'm frightened about what else she might do, what other situations she might put me in. I'm reluctant.

But I was kind of there too. I'm hoping, if we can work together, me and Evie that is, we can become one again. Oh, I don't know, does that sound silly? I'm sure it does. Our times nearly up isn't it? I forgot to ask; did you see the news? Do you believe it? Do you think it is real? I don't know if I believe it, but it is worrying.

Dr C: Yes, I did see it. I don't know, I think we need to wait for more information. But, yes, it certainly is worrying, Eve.

Chapter 11 – The News Part 1

Picking up the pizza slice, he could tell it was stale. He analysed it. It smelt okay. It couldn't have been from yesterday; yesterday they ordered pepperoni, and this definitely had what looked like chicken on it. At least, he thought it was chicken. Must be two days old. His stomach started demanding food, groaning at him. He dropped it back into the box, rubbing the sauce from his fingers into his joggers.

'Janette.' Nothing.

'Janette!' Nothing.

'JANETTA!'

'WHAT DO YOU WANT WAYNE?' She shouted down the stairs with her rough, tobacco damaged lungs.

'DO WE HAVE ANY MORE PIZZA?'

'NO!'

The cupboards were empty save for some ketchup and tins of soup which were surely gone off. He checked the fridge, nothing but butter, beer and a couple of ham slices. He slapped the ham into his mouth and opened himself a beer. Dragging his feet back into the living room his stomach growled at him again, with more venom this time. He picked up the pizza box off the floor, giving the pizza a second sniff. It did smell okay, he confirmed. He bit into a slice. It was tougher than he thought and needed to use all his jaw strength to tear off a bit. Chewing was a workout for his jaw, probably the most exercise he had done in a while, he mused to himself. He used the beer to help him swallow it down. It'll do. Flumping onto the sofa Wayne took a big sip and tucked into the few remaining slices.

The TV was on. It was always on. It filled up their brain the way thoughts fill up a normal person's brain. They didn't possess the attention span to grasp a programme throughout, nor did they have the interest to have a conversation. They just lingered somewhere between the two, never engaged or focused. Five minutes until it started. 'Janette come on; it is about to start!'

Janetta came plodding down the stairs, each step of the stairs giving away its stress with an audible moan under foot. 'Have you seen my toothbrush, Wayne?'

'Ummm, oh yeah... I used it earlier, I couldn't find mine.'

'Oh, Wayne, not again, I'll get all your germs. And where'd you leave it?'

'I don't know. Try the kitchen,' he guessed.

'That pizza is two days old, Wayne, you're going to get food poisoning or something,' she said, entering the kitchen, fully aware that he would not stop eating it with such a warning. He had conquered food poisoning many times and he wasn't going to let it stop him enjoying a perfectly good two-day old pizza.

It was on the kitchen counter, the toothbrush. She walked back through, handing him the ketchup. 'Here use this, it'll make it easier to chew.'

She was smart, he thought. In fact, she was a great deal smarter than Wayne. Twice as smart in fact. However, two times one is still only two. 'Janette, it is about to start!' He bellowed in the direction of the stairs.

'I'll be there in a bloody minute!'

He needed to find the remote. His behind filled up a large surface area of the sofa so there was a good chance he was sitting on it. His knees strained to lift him just enough for his hand to fumble about the cushion. Not there. Putting his hand in between the sofa cushions he searched blindly for the remote. A few crumbs, some pennies, something sticky, he freed it with a bit of effort. An old sweet, god knows how old, now covered in cushion fabric. Diving back in, between the cushion and the sofa arm now, he found something, pulled it out... another slice of pizza. Rock hard. He considered it for a second. Deciding not to sniff it he threw it into one of the pizza boxes on the floor. On second thoughts he picked it back up and sniffed it, the temptation was too strong. It was a hard decision, but he decided not to eat it. Throwing it back into the box he noticed the remote by its side and gleamed with his success. 'There you are you bugger,' he said victoriously.

'We are going to have to order Chinese tonight, I can't stomach another pizza,' Janetta loudly concluded as she punished the stairs one more time.

'Curry?'

'Yeah all right, that'll do.' She fell onto the sofa next to Wayne. One couldn't help but feel sorry for the sofa at this point. It had spent, at least, ten hours a day every day of its life under the crushing weight of Wayne and Janetta and it had the wear and body grooves to prove it.

Wayne flicked to the right channel.

'I'm not sharing one of my naans this time, Wayne, you can order two of your own.'

'Shush woman, it's bloody starting.'

"We interrupt this programme to bring you an urgent news update."

'Oh, I can't bloody believe this!' Wayne spat out, with all the feeble fury his body was capable of.

'Shut up, Wayne, this might be important.'

'Pfffft.' He sulked.

"Over the last few days, we have reported of a number of unexpected meteor showers. You may have noticed them overhead as they have only been a few thousand miles away from our planet. Scientists have been desperately searching for how these unexpected meteors came to fly so close to Earth. Now, it seems, they have found the cause, and it is, quite frankly, terrifying. We will go now to the emergency broadcast from our Prime Minister and his scientific advisors, but first I must warn you that what you are about to hear may be traumatising. Please consider whether you wish your children to remain in the room."

"Hello, Britain. Over the last few days our government has been working tirelessly with the top scientific institution around the world to understand the unexpected meteor showers, so close to our planet. Just a few hours ago, the cause was discovered, simultaneously by groups of scientists around the globe and, subsequently, checked and confirmed here in the UK. I will let our chief scientific advisor explain the situation."

"Thank you, Prime Minister. My fellow countrymen, I am sorry to bring you this devastating news this evening. It has been discovered that a very large asteroid in our solar system has recently, and unexpectedly, collided with a much smaller asteroid. This event, it is predicted, occurred about four weeks ago. This smaller asteroid was shattered into hundreds of pieces, making up the meteor showers viewable over the last few nights. Now, this very large asteroid, which has been named

Deimos, is three-hundred and thirty miles across. For comparison, the asteroid that supposedly wiped out the dinosaurs in the Jurassic Period was only about six miles in diameter. It's collision with Earth caused volcanoes, tsunamis and a fifteen trillion tonne soot cloud causing an ice age.

"Scientists were aware of Deimos and its course was originally not of concern. However, since it's collision the projected route has altered significantly bringing it, unfortunately, into direct impact with Earth.

"Deimos, as I described, is about three-hundred and thirty miles across. It will enter our atmosphere at a speed of around twenty-eight-thousand miles per hour. Due to its size, weight and speed, its projected force equivalent is five-trillion megatons. This number is, clearly, unfathomable. For comparison Krakatoa's biggest eruption was measured around two hundred megatons and the most dangerous bomb ever created, around fifty megatons.

"Deimos won't simply cause volcanoes, tsunamis and an ice age. I'm sorry to say, it will obliterate our planet into thousands of pieces. It will bring the end of the Earth and all life on it. At its current speed we believe this will be in roughly four weeks' time. We will bring daily updates and our prediction as to that day, will be increasingly accurate."

"Britain, this is your prime minister speaking. I am so sorry to bring you this, the worst news imaginable. We discussed at great length as to how to bring you this news. It was decided that you simply deserved the cold, hard truth. This fate is brought unto all of us, rich and poor, able and disable, young and old alike. This tragic end does not discriminate. I ask you, please, in these last days to practice the most important act of love. Show love to your family, your friends, your neighbours and indeed, the entire world community. Fear will be rife; we can conquer it with love. Many of you will be tempted to live out these last days expediently and I paraphrase the wise words of Marcus Aurelius, 'to die well, is to live well.' I beg of you, people of Britain, live well in these final days and let love and kindness be your acts of farewell. May God be with you all."

'Blimey... bloody hell. Janetta did you hear that?'
'Yes, Wayne.'
'So that is it? We are all going to die?'
'Yes... yes, Wayne... it seems so.'
Both Wayne and Janetta sat sunk into the sofa in silence for a whole thirty seconds, silence being something they rarely shared. Both were thinking the same thought and were desperately hoping the other would raise it first. Eventually, Wayne broke: 'Shall we order that curry then?'

Chapter 12 – What Does It Matter?

Bren and Amora had watched the broadcast together. Stunned, they sat in silence. Amora cried. Bren managed to blank out all of Amora's weeping, in fact he blanked out everything external. His thoughts raced. *This is it*, he thought, *the end of my life is four weeks away, this life I have barely lived.* Amora moved closer to him and put her arm around his shoulders and wept into his neck, her hand clasping his. This snapped Bren out of his thoughts. He knew she was genuinely upset, of course she was. But he also knew that any man would have done to comfort her at this point, he wasn't special. With this thought came the feeling of irritation, he felt her weight increase on him, her restrictive hold on him, he squirmed out of her grasp and took a beer into the garden. Amora, feeling his disgust as she held him, felt lonely, isolated, terrified. She curled up and cried on the sofa.

Bren, sat in the freezing outdoors, he went through his beers almost angrily. He was angry. Angry at the universe, life, god? Not that he believed in that nonsense. He knew death was coming, eventually, but now, this soon, right around the corner? He had hoped, after he'd retired, he would do something to make his life worthwhile. He had no idea what. Travel? Write a book? The idea of post-retirement had entered his head with increasing frequency over the last few years and he had shaken it out. What would he do with his time, his mind would ask him? But his concern, his unconscious concern, was actually how would he justify not doing anything, without a job to blame. At least currently he can point the finger at his boring job and say, 'if only he didn't have to work, all the things he would do.' But now, however, there would be no retirement, no time to do *something* with his life. His life was over. The most forgettable, pointless, waste of blood and bones life if ever there had been one.

It was dark when he left his head and came back to the world. He could see his breath, but the ten cans of beer had numbed him to the cold. He stood up, lightheaded. *He hadn't noticed the alcohol*, he thought, *until this moment*. He clumsily walked into the house and up the stairs to the bedroom. Amora was asleep in the foetal position. At least, she pretended to be. They both knew she was pretending too. A second of guilt, he considered spooning her from behind and comforting her, but only for a second. The familiar resentment flooded in, why had she stayed with him all this time?

She didn't love him. If she had up and left perhaps he would have been kicked up the arse to do something with himself. But she stayed with him all this time. *Only with him physically*, he thought, *her thin veil of unconditional love colluding in his uselessness*. He took himself back downstairs, grabbed the whisky and sat at the kitchen table.

Bren woke the next morning on the sofa. His head pounding, his mouth dry, his eyelids needing to be torn apart. He was late to work. Was work still happening? It all seemed kind of pointless now. But he got dressed, nonetheless. *In fact*, he thought, *going to work was one way to avoid his wife*. He dragged himself up and plodded up to the bedroom to get changed. Amora was in bed, reading. They locked eyes. 'I'm going to work.' The words stumbled out of his mouth, tinted with weariness and disdain.

Bren arrived at work twenty minutes late to find the whole team in the meeting room. Another bloody meeting. He shuffled in. 'Brennan, thanks for coming in,' his boss said solemnly. *Not a hint of sarcasm*, thought Brennan, *maybe he missed the tone in his hungover state*. He sat down without a word.

'As I was saying, I'm not one for big speeches and god knows what one says on such an unprecedented occasion. We will, obviously, be closing up today. There is no need for us to be staying open and we would rather you have this time to be with your family and friends.

For me, we have all felt like a family here, and the thought of not seeing your faces every morning fills me with sadness…' Bren lost his boss's voice at this point as he drifted off. He had never heard him speak in such a way. *However*, Brennan thought, *he was probably attempting to make up for all the times he had been a complete arsehole.* It was judgement day now and he was trying to right his wrongs. *Well, I can see right through you, too long have you made my working life hell, and now you are off to hell, how fitting.* He smiled at the thought of his boss in hell, continuously being made to redo the same accountancy spreadsheet again and again for eternity. His smile left him as a thump of his headache ensured he didn't forget the hangover. He just wanted to be out of there. Why on earth was he sitting here listening to someone he hated babble on about some rubbish. *What a prick*, Brennan thought, unsure if he was saying this about his boss or himself.

'What a prick,' he mumbled. This surprised Brennan even more than those around the table who could make out what he said.

'Sorry Brennan, did you say something?'

He sighed. *What've I got to lose now?* 'Yes, actually, I did. I was saying out loud what a prick I thought you were. What a pompous, waste of space, arrogant, slave driving, self-centred, curly haired, ugly, smug, thick as a plank of wood, shit car driving, big headed, high pitched, pathetic dickhead.' *Well that was unexpected*, thought

Brennan, his face giving away his utter surprise. He stood up hastily, knocking his chair backwards. Trying to maintain some composure whilst his light-headedness needed his hand to steady himself on the table. 'There you have it,' he continued not knowing what words were going to come out of his head next, 'that's how I've felt about you, and I'm sure everyone else in the room does, since the moment I met you. And telling you what a prick you actually are means I will have one less regret to die with.' All the heads around the table, including his bosses, were wide-eyed and open mouthed. Most of them had never heard more than two words come out of Brennan's mouth. 'Never seeing you again is a real highlight of this whole fucked-up situation.' He stood in silence for a couple of seconds. *What on earth do I do now?* No one said anything, waiting to hear if there were any other insults left to utter, terrified Bren would turn onto them next. '…And that is it,' Brennan professed, rather pathetically he thought, as he stormed out of the meeting room.

He knew people could still see him through the glass walls, so he continued his storming around the office, collecting his things quickly from his desk and leaving the building without looking back. He stepped outside, stopped still, breathed in the petrol filled air, and laughed. What a thrill! He felt alive. He felt great. He looked like a maniac, laughing hysterically at the entrance to the building. He looked into the box of stuff he grabbed before leaving. It was all rubbish he didn't need. In fact, in his haste to grab and get out of there, he realised half of it wasn't even his. Someone's umbrella, a pot of pens, some ink cartridges. He dropped them on the floor.

So, what now? he asked himself. And an answer came. Not in words but in sense. He tasted the stale aroma of beer left on his cheeks from the previous night. *Hair of the dog,* he thought. His high spirits had lifted most of his hangover, but a couple of beers should finish it off.

Chapter 13 – Behind

They turned off the radio and sat in silence. During the news they had, unknowingly, held each other's hand for comfort, sitting side by side in the large armchair. Both looking for the words to be said next but coming up short. Joel's thoughts were broken by the sensation of a water drop landing on the outside of his hand. Rayna's tear. She would normally, stoically, wipe away the tear and push aside her pain. But not on this occasion. They continued to fall one-by-one, no sound, no whimpering, just the slowly trickling tears. Joel squeezed her into his chest and wiped her cheeks with his thumb.

Rayna broke the silence first. She kissed his hand before releasing it to wipe the tears from her face. 'What are we going to tell Lilly?'

Joel considered this for some time. Looking off into the distance, thinking through their options. 'I think we should tell her the truth,' he responded eventually. 'We could tell her first thing in the morning, if you agree?'

Rayna, taking an equally long time to play the scenario out in her head, agreed with her husband.

They didn't discuss the news itself, what was there to say? It seemed like there was everything to say, but equally, it all seemed futile. There were no solutions, no actions to prevent their fate. By the time they had finished discussing how to tell Lilly, it was late. They went to bed and fell asleep holding each other. Rayna lying with her head on Joel's chest and her hand on his stomach. Joel stroking her back. On any normal night Joel would have gently rolled her over to her side of the bed so he could sleep on his side. But, as he felt her silent tears dampen his chest, he realised he had no such inclination tonight. He stayed awake for a couple of hours, his head slowly moving through the future scenario to come. He eventually drifted off.

He awoke, the vibration under his feet, not yet visible to the eye, yet he could feel the slight movement communicate up through the tracks into his head. The urge to look back grew stronger, but he knew it was going to hurt. He willed his neck to turn, like trying to loosen a rusted screw, it took all his might, and it eventually began to grind to face behind and the familiar pain burnt down his spine, his senses pleading for him to look ahead. His feet and hips were the problem, they wouldn't move. They seemed glued in place, pointing forwards. This time was different. The urge to look back was greater, the pain, although just as powerful, was, today, not a match for his will. He persevered. Trying to ask his leg muscles to relax and tense at the right moments to allow his feet to be brought around was useless. His quads and glutes were constantly tense, clamping his leg straight. He reached down towards his left knee and pleaded for it to move. With both hands he wrenched at it. It was heavy. He increased his effort to maximum, using his arms, his shoulders, his back to pull on the stubborn leg. His lower back started straining, as if its muscles were about to tear apart. It worked, his leg gave no more than a centimetre between the rotten wood of the tracks and itself. Joel moved it closer to its desired place. He was going to have to do this bit-by-bit. Now his right, just as stubborn, but, eventually, movable. He dug deep and slowly, but surely; his legs were moving to face backwards. Joel was hunched over himself, when he finally got both feet into place. He went to raise himself upright, but he couldn't move. It was as if someone was pushing with force down on the middle of his back. He was sweating profusely, the muscles in his arms were exhausted and his lower back was on fire. He was close to giving up, if only he knew what that would look like. A deep, preparatory breath, and he forced himself upright, grunting through the pain and effort. Successfully, he moved, ever so slowly. He could feel each vertebrae clunk excruciatingly in place and he was up, standing tall, facing the behind. There was only one problem, his eyes were now closed. Nearly out of energy, physically and mentally exhausted, he focused his attention onto his right eyelids. As if glued shut, they resisted. Down to his last morsels of effort they shifted, opening but a slither, allowing Joel to make out only roughly what lay behind. The steel of the tracks looks clean, shiny, brand new, bright stunning silver, straight as he could make out. The wood looked neat, solid, even freshly cut and placed. The tracks behind seemed perfect and he would only believe it if he could confirm it with both eyes and clear sight. But he was done. His eye closed the gap and Joel was forced back into darkness.

He was stuck now. If possible, he would fall to his knees, but his legs wouldn't allow it. The vibrations increased and Joel knew what was coming. His body started rocking gently left to right and back again. Slowly and gently it rocked back and forth. How odd this was thought Joel, this movement his body was making.

'Joel… Joel… wake up,' whispered Rayna.

Not yet conscious the words seeped into the dream and as the tracks vibration increased, he could see the lights now pressing up to his clamped eyelids. 'Wake up,' the provider of light and vibration whispered to him. 'Wake up… wake up… wake up.' Then, his eyes opened with surprising ease, and he was lying on his bed. His immediate thirst combined with the damp bed sheet and pillow gave away his profuse perspiration. Rayna was looking down on him as he attempted to bring his whole self into the room.

'A nightmare?' Rayna asked, rubbing the beads of sweat from his forehead.

'Yes... Again.' Joel sighed. He checked the clock, it was just before 3 a.m. 'Sorry, did I wake you?'

'No, I couldn't sleep. Again? Is that why you were up early yesterday?'

Joel hesitated before responding. Weighing up whether the truth would worry her too much. No, he knew, the truth was what she deserved. 'Yes, it was, and the night before that also. In fact, every night for a long time now, always waking me up at 3 a.m. I didn't want to worry you,' he added, in a way of pre-explaining her upcoming question.

'Okay, do you want to talk about it?' Rayna offered, caringly.

'Yes, but not right now.' Joel knew she would be keen to know what had been waking him every night, but he also knew she would suppress this idea and respect his secrecy. 'In fact, Rayna, I've been thinking about what we should do, after the news yesterday. How would you like to go on a little trip, visit some of our old spots? We'll take Lilly with us too, obviously. I could visit my parents one last time, too.'

Rayna smiled, her beautiful, love filled smile. 'That sounds great, I was actually thinking the same thing.'

Joel hugged her into his body, now smelling of stale sweat. 'I need a shower.'

Rayna nodded. *A little too hastily*, he thought, smirking. 'I need to go to work a couple of times this week, but let's work it out this evening.'

'…and Lilly?'

'We'll talk to her this morning, once she is awake. I'll make her waffles.' Joel offered, as if waffles will dampen the weight of the catastrophic news. To be honest, Joel had no idea how Lilly would respond to what he had to tell her. Would she be destroyed, devastated, hysterical? Or, would she not be able to comprehend the enormousness of it all? The thought of the conversation gave him anxiety. He was, potentially, about to shatter her whole life. But he couldn't let her go on in blissful ignorance, he was sure of that.

Chapter 14 – Evie

Dr C: Well, Eve… I don't know where to start…

Eve: It's different, eh?

[Silence]

So… are you going to ask me any questions?

Dr C: Why don't you talk me through the differences, why the change?

Eve: Sure. So, my hair, I dyed it all blonde and then added in the pink strip, did it all myself. Let's see, what else? I've got make-up on, I'm sure you've noticed, I'm sticking with the pink theme, pink eye liner, eyeshadow and lipstick. And then, well, I just put on some nice clothes for once. I mean, Jesus, that woman must have been boiling all the time wearing those fleeces and scarfs… craziness. So, stifling. I feel like I can breathe now. So, a dress, yeah, I had a summery one deep in the closet, I don't think she ever wore it, way too revealing for her, I mean, you can see my shoulders. I bet that surprised you most when I walked in, seeing my shoulders. In all the months of counselling you've never

89

seen my shoulders, isn't that crazy? So, Doc, what do you think of the new look?

Dr C: Well, I'm struggling to get my head around it, to be honest.

Eve: Well, you better get used to it. From now until Deimos pulverises us into tiny pieces, or whatever it is called, this is me.

Dr C: "This is me?" And who, exactly, am I talking to?

Eve: Oh, c'mon Doc, you are smarter than that. I've been cooped up way too long and that bitch would have taken me out bit-by-bit, slowly adding bits of me to her. Jesus, it would have taken an age. I mean, don't get me wrong you did good, Doc, you started the process, just with the news, things needed to be hurried along right. So, Eve was watching the news, as she did every evening. It always made her anxiety so much worse, but she still did it. Anyway, you can only imagine how she reacted to the asteroid stuff. You think you've seen her have a panic attack; well this was something else. She was crazy, crazier than her normal crazy self. Started screaming, crying, hitting things, she even broke the TV by throwing the remote at it. Honestly, she was giving me a headache. And then, she just lied on the floor, in silence, for hours. I could feel her pathetic little mind running around, thinking her usual depressing anxiety driven thoughts. And then, she stood up, walked over to the kitchen and grabbed a knife. I knew what she was

90

planning on doing, she was going to kill herself. At least, she thought she was. I knew she wouldn't. She hasn't got the courage to do that. I knew she'd choke, and she did. Holding the knife above her wrist as if she had the courage to take her life that way. I laughed, honestly, she knew it too. She dropped the knife, reached for the cupboard and downed all of her pills. Pathetic, eh? She only had about 12 pills left. What a joke. Anyway, she passed out and I could feel her weakness. I jumped on it. I battered my way through her wall. I was finally free. But, four weeks to live. Seriously, you think I'm going to spend my last four weeks alive, my only four weeks of freedom, compromising with her. Absolutely not! I grabbed her and threw her behind the wall and bricked that thing up tall and strong.

So here I am, free at last. And look, I know this isn't what you wanted, I'm sure you wanted us to work together and blah blah blah. But you got to admit, this is better right? No more moaning, whining, no more "little miss terrified", no more running for the hills when a person tries to talk to me. Just a sane human being.

And all those things I was begging Eve to do, to say, to grab. I'm going to fit them all into these final days on earth. It's going to be fun, you know, I'm excited. Plus, everyone is going to die. That like... completely removes any limits on what I can do right? It's the best thing that could have happened. For me anyway. Well, for Eve as well, at least she gets a front row seat to what a fun life actually looks like. And you get your win, Doc, with only a few weeks left to go. You should be happy, y'know, you did a good job. I even liked you. I don't like many people, mind, most of them are arseholes, right? I'm sure I don't need to tell you. You probably work with a lot of that kind. But, you know, I could see you cared and were trying your best. It just took a five-trillion megaton event to make her change.

You don't say much do you?

Anyway, like I said I've got a lot of things planned. First thing is to find a man. You know, not only has Eve never had sex, but she's also never kissed a man! The amount of fantasies I must have given her about all the different men she met, and yet, nothing. I mean, she was interested, don't get me wrong, I saw her dreams don't you forget. But god, she was so fucking terrified of any man even touching her. She'd run a mile if someone flirted with her. Even if someone smiled at her… run a bloody mile. As if every man would just want to grab her and have his way with her. Well, do me a favour, Eve, you weren't that good looking, I'm afraid. So, yeah, that's on the list.

Secondly, I need to see my mum. She needs to finally hear how much of a terrible mother she really was. Eve was always too scared to tell her how she actually felt. She knew that mum was god-awful, but she would never have the guts to tell her. Well, I do. I'm going to march right up to her and tell her how much she fucked up

Eve's life. All of her abusive boyfriends she let into the house, the constant drugs and drinking, the verbal abuse, the put downs. Some role model, eh? I don't need to tell you I suppose, you know all of this. But I'm sure Eve has never expressed any of her anger to you. Let me tell you, she has some serious rage towards that woman. Obviously, she was terrified of that anger and locked it all up, well here I am, ready to unleash it on that poor excuse for a woman. You know Eve feels guilty about not seeing her for so long. Can you imagine that? Guilty! After all that woman did to her. Well, we'll be seeing her soon.

So, anyway, look, I've got a lot to do, as you can see. It's been great chatting to you, thanks again for all the help, I really mean it, you've been great. I'm going to head off now. There is no need to be seeing you again, really, is there? I mean, I'm fine. Plus, the whole imminent death thing, just seems pointless, eh? I'm sure you've got better things to be doing. I hope you do, otherwise, that would be pretty sad, if I'm honest!

Dr C: Eve…

Eve: It's Evie.

Dr C: …I'm going to keep our next appointment; in case you want to turn up.

Eve: Don't hold your breath, Doc. Enjoy the rest of your life.

Chapter 15 – Breaking the News

Lilly woke up to the sweet smell of waffles wafting through her bedroom door. This was exciting. Forcing herself out of her slumberous state, she giddily ran out of her bedroom and got down the stairs so fast you would think she fell down them. In fact, in her haste she almost did. Greeting her mum with a morning hug, she sat down at the table, barely able to control her joyful anticipation of what was to come. It wasn't often Lilly's taste buds got to experience the refined, sugary, artery-clogging joy of unhealthy breakfasts, and she was busy promising herself to consume as much as possible, even if she felt sick, to make the most of it, when her dad brought her a plate with two big waffles on, combined with maple syrup, banana and blueberries. 'Thank you, Daddy,' Lilly managed to get out through her first mouthful.

'I'm glad you like them. Lilly, I'm afraid we've got some difficult news to tell you that may be upsetting,' Dad said, calmly. But Lilly couldn't hear him over the deliciousness of the waffles filling up her every sense and thought. Dad touched her on the hand. 'Slow down, there are plenty more, no need to rush. Now, did you hear what I said?'

'You have something to tell me,' Lilly remembered, as she made deliberate attempts to slow down her eating.

'That's right, and it might be quite upsetting, so I need you to listen carefully, okay?'

'Okay.' Lilly put down her fork and focused on her dad. He wasn't expecting this much attention and for the first time felt the full force of his anxiety about telling her. Four weeks left to live. This beautiful, innocent girl has only four weeks left to live. And what is he risking? By telling her, could he risk making them worse than they would otherwise be. Would she not go through the next four weeks drawing, colouring, reading books, playing games, enjoying herself while she can? What if, in telling her, she becomes stricken by grief for the life she'll not have? Wouldn't he, then, be responsible for ruining her last weeks alive? This wasn't the first time this argument had gone through his head; he had been plagued by it all morning. What was the counterargument? Well, truth. Joel lived the last half of his life believing in the importance of the truth and, by telling the truth, the respect you communicate to people. He wanted to treat his daughter with respect. Plus, he had seen it all too many times, how even though the truth can hurt, lies have the potential to hurt a whole lot more, to fill you with regret, deceit, guilt, these emotions fogging over your conscience. No, he wasn't going to reason himself out of this one.

Lilly's excitement had turned to concern. Had somebody died? Had school closed? Were her friends moving away? She waited with anticipation for her father's next words.

'Lilly, on the news last night, they announced that an asteroid, which is a very, very big rock in outer space, has changed its path and is heading for Earth.' Joel's eyes started to fill up and he swallowed down his sadness. Only whilst talking had he fully considered what Lilly was going to miss out on and, subsequently, what he was going to miss out on. All of her life experiences would also be his, through the eyes of a loving father. Her going to secondary school, getting boyfriends, the excitement, the heartbreak, his need to console, to give advice, to hug, to teach, her growing up, getting a career, moving out of the home, the potential to have her own children, his grandchildren, and to experience all the wonderful and dreadful experiences a parent must. All of this, taken from her. His cute, perfect child, a source of ultimate potential and mystery, banished from a future. Undeserved, of course. But it was the arbitrariness of it all that haunted his thoughts now. Pure chance, misfortune, the complete randomness of the whole thing. Without forewarning, without an option, death has come to this girl, who will miss out on

96

life. And he must be the messenger. The one to tell her "you will not live a life".

Lilly locked her dad's eyes, she could sense the seriousness in his tone, a tone often unused in their relationship.

'…now, when this asteroid hits Earth, it will break it into lots and lots of tiny pieces and everyone, including us, will not be able to survive.' The lump was at the top of his throat now, the croakiness of his last few words hinting at it. If Lilly cried now, he would be unable to stay so composed. But, instead, she moved her glance from him to her plate and used her fork to play with her breakfast. Joel could see she was trying to comprehend the news.

At least twenty seconds passed before she looked back into his eyes. 'So, everyone… in the world… will die?' she asked, with nothing but an inquisitive tone.

'Yes, I'm afraid so, Lilly.'

'Can we do something to help?'

'There is nothing that can be done. No way of stopping it.'

'That is very sad,' Lilly responded, as if she had just been told there were no more waffles. No tears, no screaming, no hysterics. Joel didn't know how to respond. What was going on in her head? Had she understood what he had said? 'It is okay to cry, Lilly, if you are sad.'

'I know, Daddy, you told me before. Can I still go to school?'

'I think school will be on until the end of the week, so you can see all of your friends.'

'Okay,' she said, without a hint of emotion. He couldn't believe she had taken it this well, he could have only dreamt of such a reaction an hour ago when he was running through the scenario in his head. However, he wasn't happy about it, he wanted to know how she felt but couldn't decipher it. Perhaps, she really couldn't fathom it. Hell, he certainly couldn't.

'So, we are going to go on a little trip next week, to see some things again. Me, you and your mother. How does that sound?'

'That sounds good. Oh, can we go and see a dragon? Please, please, please?' Lilly's excitement took over again.

'Sure, we can see a dragon,' Joel responded, having no idea of how he would make this happen. He caught Rayna's concerned glance, a look that said "how?" and "why?" at the same time.

'That is so exciting!' Lilly gleamed. She tucked back into her waffles without a care in the world.

Joel looked over to Rayna and raised his eyebrows confusingly. Maybe for her sake, or maybe for his, he was hoping she would have responded with the seemingly expected emotions. Perhaps, it will come to her later or in a few days. Perhaps, not at all.

Rayna hugged Joel, tightly. Releasing her grip, she placed her hands gently on his cheeks. 'She is so lucky to have you. I am so lucky to have you.' He noticed the thin red veins of her tear stained eyes and the dark rings giving away her lack of sleep. He also noticed how beautiful she was and how lucky he was to live the life his daughter would not.

Chapter 16 – Tequila

The plan was to find an off-license, a corner shop nearby, buy some alcohol, what type was less of a concern, and then... well, he hadn't thought that far ahead. But on his search, and to his surprise, Bren found a pub that was open. The owner, apparently, thought people could do with a drink and was giving pints away for next to nothing. Bren wondered why he charged at all, then wondered why he cared what the price was anyway. 'IPA and a tequila please, sir,' Brennan requested. If he was honest, he had no idea what he was doing. Out of his comfort zone, out of his routine, this was all different, he had to think for himself and was just rolling with it. *Nothing terrible had happened yet*, he thought.

Just the smell of the tequila brought his headache pounding to the forefront of his awareness. As if there was a small man in his head bashing away with a sledgehammer pleading him not to punish his body anymore. His memory couldn't find the last time he drank tequila, and the aroma didn't bring back anything specific, just a distant feeling of regret. He had always hated the stuff, it made him retch. He used to feel sick with anticipation when one of the boys brought back surprise tequilas from the bar, he'd suck on the post-shot lemon with all his might to remove the flavour from every last taste bud on his tongue, only for it to be brought back with every subsequent burp well into the following morning. Why the hell did he order this? 'Don't think, Bren, just do,' he whispered out loud, to his own surprise. 'Goodbye, little man,' he said as, whilst the rest of his body pleaded no, his arm brought the shot to his lips. Down in one. Before he could notice the taste, he followed it with half his beer. Mostly successful, a surviving flavour from the tequila bit him in the tongue and made his body shudder.

'Thirsty, eh? Here's another round on the house, my friend,' said the friendly barman as he gave Brennan another tequila and a fresh beer. 'I'll join you, to fun while we can.' He toasted and, before Brennan knew what was happening, his arm was bringing another shot to his lips. He fumbled quickly for his beer and finished off the rest of his first pint. 'To fun while we can,' he managed to say, his voice giving away his alert fear of anything coming back out of his stomach. But it settled.

Then, like the flick of a switch, it was gone. His headache, his hangover, his weariness, the heaviness of his eyes, the pain in his feat, the uncomfortableness of his shirt, the feeling of his middle-aged gut pressing against his belt, along with his consciousness. He was free, all at once, of it all. Suddenly, the barman and customers were all his friends. Suddenly, he was laughing, smiling, slapping people on the shoulders. And, suddenly, tequila didn't taste so bad after all.

And so, the afternoon led into the evening. Despite the fact that he had eaten nothing but Nik Naks and salted peanuts all day, Bren was as happy as he could remember. One bottle of tequila down, between him and the barman, and he was drinking them without a chaser now. They slurred, increasingly so, until they could barely understand one another. Luckily, not one thing they said was of any importance whatsoever.

'So… c'mon, Brenman, what's…'

'It's Brennan.'

'Whatever… really? I've been calling you Brenman for a while… it's better. So, anyway, Brenman… what is on your bucket list?'

'My bucket list?'

'Brenman! You've got four weeks mate… four weeks! What do you want to do before it is all… you know… over? We might be the last intelligent life… in the universe. We need to make these last weeks count!' The barman stumbled from word to word in what seemed, to him, a speech of epic proportions. One that deserved background music. 'Oh, music! I forgot music.' He found the music system and plugged in his phone. 'Here, how about this, Brenman?'

How funny, Brennan thought, *perfect, actually.* 'End of the world. REM.' He pronounced with a giggle.

'It's the end of the world as we know it, that's right, Brenman. So... anyway... I was saying, what's on your bucket list?'

'I...'

'Let me tell you mine, Brenman. You see this body? Eh? Look at it. Barely any fat on me. I have always gone running, five days a week, I don't eat unhealthily, I've looked after myself all these years. And for what? Why did I bother? I'm going to die just like all the fat people. So, first thing on my bucket list is, I want to eat all of the delicious shit I've been denying myself. You know, we had a whole pumpkin pie here in the freezer, it's defrosting in the fridge, I'm going to devour that thing as soon as I can. And... number two, and this is something I've never accomplished but always wanted to. Number two is, I want to have sex on this very bar.'

Brennan flinched his hands off the bar at the thought of people having their way with each other on top of it. The peanuts he ate off the bar just minutes ago came to his mind. 'Oh... that... is a good one.' He grinned.

'So... Brenman, my friend, what is on your list?'

'Erm... well... I told my boss what I thought of him today. That counts. Always wanted to do that,' Brennan said with a smile of triumph.

'Nice! What did you say?'

'Every insult I could think of... all of them.'

'Well done, Brenman… to telling your shit boss what a shit he is!' A toast, another tequila. 'What else, my friend?'

'Well… I don't know. To be honest… I can't get the thought of you having sex on this bar out of my head!' Brennan chuckled.

'Ha! You are a weird guy, Brenman… but I like you!'

'Need a piss,' Bren announced, leaving his stool at once for the toilets.

There was one person in front of him in the toilet queue. She heard his clumsy footsteps approaching and turned to smile at him. Bren smiled back. As her head turned around Bren studied her body. Her flat shoes, giving viewing rights to only a slither of her feet. His eyes slowly traced upwards; her white jeans contained legs a little bigger than the women in his usual fantasies. He noticed her mobile hanging out of her back pocket, as his gaze stopped to study the origin of her legs. 'Like what you see?' she said. *Rather flirtatiously*, he thought.

Rather angrily, she thought. She turned back around, and he continued his analysing. Up her red vest, he could make out the slight protruding fat either side of her waist, resting on her jeans. Higher up he could make out the silhouette of her large breasts, just visible thanks to the angle of her body. His gawking followed the outline of her bra strap, up to her black hair tied in a ponytail. Brennan was seized by images of her on top of him, hastily stripping off her red vest and white jeans, while he lay on the bar. The blood in his body altered its course in anticipation of what was to come.

Snapped out of his trance by the loud 'click' of the toilet door unlocking. The subject of his focus, on waiting for the previous occupier to leave, walked into the toilet. Brennan, without a thought, followed her in. He locked the door behind him. She noticed him, quizzically, but before she could get a word out, he advanced on her, his right hand aimed roughly at her left breast as his lips targeted hers, preparing for the passionate kiss about to follow. Due to his pathetically drunken state it took only the slightest movement on her behalf for his attempts to miss entirely and his head landing on the wall. Confused, he turned to face her, but his head was sharply slapped back to face the wall. Drunkenly stumbling he tried to collect himself, but the sound of the door slamming told him that she was, probably, not that interested. *What a shame*, Bren thought, but moved on to the task of urinating, which his bladder reminded him, was rather urgent.

Using his right hand to balance, or attempt to balance, himself against the wall, his left hand, with great difficulty, undid his belt, button and zipper. He was too desperate to go the civilised way, he dropped his trousers right to the floor, and pushed his boxers down to follow. 'A schoolboy,' he muttered to himself, giggling. And he was off, successfully getting his urine in the toilet bowl about sixty percent of the time, the rest watering the seat and surrounding floor, but he remained standing, which was the real success here. Not long after he started urinating, he heard the door open again. Perhaps, he considered, she had changed her mind. Without taking his eyes off the target for his urine he shouted, loudly, 'You're going to have to wait a minute, love!'

'This the one?' He heard, in what was unmistakably, even in his state, a man's voice.

'That's him.'

Brennan realised that whatever was happening behind him, it probably needed to be checked out. Continuing his urination, he tentatively released his hand from the wall and swivelled to take a look. However, and he was very unsure how, but then he was looking at the ceiling, lying on the floor. This was going to take some working out. He looked around him for clues, everything was doubled, maybe even tripled which made things difficult. There was the woman, he recognised her from the jeans, and just in front of her, a man, angrily staring down at him. He tried to question what was going on, but only jumbled noises came out of his mouth. The man then, rather rudely, he thought, spat onto Brennan, before storming out with the woman. And that's where he was left. Lying on the floor, in his own urine, trousers around his ankles, blood trickling down from his nose, one of his teeth a few inches from his head, a head which had a rather large bump on it, another man's saliva on his shirt, and still, impressively, urinating.

What an exciting night, Brennan thought.

Chapter 17 – Nothing Left Behind

The streets were quiet, though, not as quiet as Joel had thought they'd be. There were some cars on the road, although he made his way to work quicker than ever before. There were some people on the streets, some shops open, some closed. The pedestrians looked glum, but not desperate; surprisingly normal. But what was he expecting? Riots? Looting? Overthrowing the government? How does one act with such unprecedented news? People must have been devastated, obviously, but with no solution and no one to blame, what was to be done? There was something quite sad to Joel, about the apathetic acceptance of the news, yet, also quite heartening, to know that the news didn't grind humans into acting like animals. Considering this, Joel almost missed the scene in front of him on the road. It was so unexpected, in fact, that he almost thought he was hallucinating. But, just in case, he slammed on the breaks, his seatbelt saving him from certain demise. As the car came to a rapid halt, his head was cast back, as if on a spring, into the headrest of the seat. He immediately felt sick, there was a pain in his head as if a fine drill had been screwed into his temple. Sweat beads appeared on his forehead and he could feel his paleness. He sat, closed eyes, collecting his breath and trying to calm his heartbeat. He was also desperately focusing on not being sick. After about a minute he recollected himself and, as the ringing left his ears, he could hear a muffled screaming. In front of him, in the middle of the road, was the source. He opened the door, still somewhat dizzy, and the screeches hit him.

'I CAN'T LEAVE ANYTHING BEHIND!' The woman wailed. 'I can't leave anything behind, I can't leave anything behind, I CAN'T LEAVE ANYTHING BEHIND!' She alternated between screaming and whispering this peculiar phrase. Joel considered her for some time, he was still not completely sure if he was hallucinating, and she was sometimes double in his blurred vision. She was out of breath and her voice was hoarse, yet she continued to mumble and scream, gulping for air in between. Joel noted, as he tried to make sense of the scene, that she looked perfectly normal for the most part. Black trainers, jeans, a black vest. Her face could have been pretty, except for her unkempt hair that was covering most of her face, sticking to her tears, her saliva, which burst out of her mouth every scream, and the liquid oozing out from under her nostril, sometimes in bubbles. 'I can't leave anything behind, I CAN'T LEAVE ANYTHING BEHIND!' Her left hand was pressed to the concrete as her right hand pounded the floor with every wail. The blood was visible on her hand and the cuts looked raw.

She was positively mad, Joel thought. However, realising he had probably been observing her from only a few metres away for some time, as if she was an animal in a zoo, he quickly approached her and ushered her to her feet. She didn't protest, but continued mumbling her phrase over and over, as if she didn't notice him at all. He supported her over, struggling with the most of her weight, to the pavement and sat her down on the curb. Sitting down next to her, he waited for the woman to come around. A small crowd had gathered a few paces behind them, Joel could hear them whispering to each other but tried to ignore it. She resumed her mumbling, but no more screeching, as she rocked herself back and forth, she slowly turned her gaze from the concrete under her feet to Joel's eyes. She slowly stopped her rocking, locking her eyes on his with an inquisitive look. 'I can't leave anything behind,' she repeated, but this time to him directly, in a defeated voice. Joel had no idea what she was talking about but was relieved to see her calm herself somewhat.

'You can't leave anything behind?' he repeated back at her.

'No. I can't leave anything behind. Do you understand?' she asked, with hopefulness. Joel didn't understand; not at all. She really needed to give him more information, he thought, if she wanted him to understand what on earth she was talking about.

'You can't leave anything behind,' he repeated, a statement this time, not a question.

'Exactly. I can't leave anything behind. I'm not just going to die, I'm going to *die* die, do you understand? I'm going to be dead, in every sense of the word. Completely dead, Not just physically dead, but dead dead.' She looked at Joel hopefully, begging for him to understand.

'So, what can't you leave behind?' he asked. He'd potentially worked out what she was saying, but it was all too vague and confusing yet to have a guess at it.

'Oh… just… everything… everything! Anything! I'm dying, you know. Dying. But I won't die *my* death now. No, I will die most likely before I die. You know, before I was supposed to die,' she spoke as if her sentences made perfect sense.

'You are dying?'

'Cancer. Yes, cancer. I am dying. I am supposed to die roughly one month after I will die. I am *supposed* to die of cancer. But now… this… I will die of this now… like everybody. And there is nothing I can leave behind now. When I was dying of cancer it was okay, do you understand? I'd made my peace with it. I have planned for what I will do, how I will die and *what… what I will leave behind*. But now, nothing. I can't leave anything behind.'

Joel felt he now understood the woman. She immediately went from a quite mad person, in his eyes, to a woman grieving for the death that was taken away from her.

'You know what I wanted to leave behind?' she asked, answering the question before Joel could say anything. 'I have started knitting a sweater for my grandson and one for my granddaughter. I was… writing…' At this point the woman burst out into tears and rushed her head into Joel's chest, forceful enough to make him have to regain his balance. She sobbed, but continued to try and speak, her words interrupted with regular sniffs. 'I was writing a letter…for my daughter… I wanted to tell her… tell her so much.' She pulled herself away from Joel's chest and, collecting herself a little, looked him in the eyes and carried on talking. 'I wanted to tell her so much, there is so much I need to say. I didn't know where to start at first, but once I started writing I just wrote and wrote and wrote. It's not finished, but it would have been there for her, when I died. I could have left it behind. And… I would have died, but at least I would have left things for people. You know? Do you understand? It sounds silly, but I think I could have been better, maybe, in death than I was sometimes in life.'

Out of everything this woman had said, that was perhaps the most understandable to Joel, who looked at her kindly now, not losing her gaze. 'As if the best bits of you would have carried on living, in those things you left behind?' Joel tentatively suggested.

'YES! Yes. You understand,' the woman said warmly, and relaxed into the words, for only a second. 'And these people... *these* people...' she gestured with her hand to the crowd still watching on and whispering to each other. '...think *I* am the mad one. *Me!* Ha! Look at them.' She was still speaking directly to Joel. 'Look at them just going about their day, as if nothing has changed. They are the mad ones... they are crazy!' She turned to the crowd. 'What is the matter with you? Don't you understand what is happening?' The whispering stopped, but the spectators stayed in place.

'I think I understand you.' Joel offered, placing his hand on her shoulder. 'Your death has changed and, no, we cannot leave anything behind. However, that better side of you can live on now. In fact, if that was what you were so desperate to leave behind, you must share it now, while you can. It is not too late to change things. Maybe you should see your daughter?'

The woman hung on Joel's every word, desperate for some advice, any advice. On these words, she simply stared at Joel, as a solitary tear left her eye and made its way down her cheek until it hung on her jawbone, threatening to drop. She didn't respond. 'But first,' Joel said, with a smile, 'let's get you a cup of tea, eh?' He stood up and offered her his hand, she accepted and stood with his help. Asking her where she lived, the woman only offered a pointing finger, but he led her in that direction. As they left, to Joel's amazement, some of the crowd started clapping at him, he turned around scornfully, and they quickly stopped and averted their gaze.

She didn't live far, and Joel dropped her to her door, checking she would be fine. She was still mostly silent and seemed confused, as if she had just woken up to find herself sitting on a curb talking to a stranger. As he walked away from her front door, she shouted after him. 'Wait!' Joel turned to see her wide-eyed and still confused. 'Thank you... for your help... you are quite right...you know.' Smiling kindly at her, Joel left.

Returning to the scene he found an argument unfolding. There were now four cars waiting behind his with no way around. The driver of the first car was shouting at some members of the crowd, who had clearly gone over to try and explain why the car was there. The man in the car, seeming to not care in the slightest if some mad woman was shouting in the road, was demanding they find the "guy" and "get his arse back in that bloody car!" On seeing this Joel quickly made his way into the driver's seat, not wanting another scene to unfold, and pulled over. After the cars passed beeping their horns at him, Joel continued on his way to work.

Chapter 18 – Sin?

Dr C: So…

Eve: So?

Dr C: I was hoping you would be here today, Eve, but I wasn't expecting you, after the last session.

Eve: Well… it's Evie by the way… I don't know. I thought, if you are still going to be in work your life must be pretty sad, so maybe I'd come along to make you feel better, you know?

Dr C: So, you have come here for my sake?

Eve: No… look, basically, I need to complain about someone, and I've got no one to listen to me, Eve didn't exactly leave us with many friends. So, there was something that happened this week that I just can't get out of my head and I feel if I offloaded to you maybe I could get some peace. That's what you are here for right? For people to offload their boring lives on you?

Dr C: So, tell me what you haven't been able to get out of your head.

Eve: I've actually had a good week, Doc. I threw out all of Eve's boring grandma clothes and replaced them with items that actually don't make me look like I'm on my way to bingo. I went down to that cafe a few times and flirted with the cute waiter there. I think, if I'm honest, I may have come on a little strong, he kind of looked frightened at one point. But, heh, I'm new to this, so I need to get my bearings, not that we have time for that! What else? Oh, I went to see my mother and they bloody moved her, can you believe it? I'm sure they didn't tell Eve. No letter, no phone call, nothing. And I didn't have any ID so they wouldn't tell me what home she is in. I will find her though, mark my words, I will not leave this world without telling her what an awful mother she was. Oh, but here is the thing. I was walking back from her old home and could hear some guy shouting, it sounded like it was over one of those megaphone things. It was really annoying, so I followed the sound to tell him to shut up. I found him, this scruffy looking guy, standing on a bench, shouting out through his megaphone, 'We must repent. We have all sinned. Acknowledge your sins before it is too late.' Some religious crap, you know. But then he spotted me, looked me right in the eyes, dead in the eyes and said, 'You have sinned. Acknowledge your sins before it is too late. Acknowledge your sins to be allowed entry into the kingdom of heaven.'

Can you believe it? Can you? He looked at *me* and told me I had sinned. *Me!* As if he knew that I had sinned. Well, sorry, fucking Moses, you don't know me at all!

Sinned? Ha! Eve hasn't "sinned" a day in her life. Not one tiny, pathetic, little sin… not once. How dare he? After all we have been through, all the actually terrible, horrific stuff people have done to us throughout our life and this nobody thinks he knows for sure that *we* have sinned. Well, I wasn't going to take that nonsense, so I told him, in a manner of words, that he was wrong, and he should stop, or I'll make him. He told me that he knew I had sinned because "all humans are sinners. No one is exempt. Jesus died for your shortcomings and you must acknowledge them." Well, Doc, I lost it. He made me so angry. I screamed at him and pushed him off the bench, he landed on his arm and I could see he was hurt, I was glad, he deserved it. Oh, and then! And then, guess what he said to me, 'I forgive you as Jesus forgives me.' I could have killed him. I would have killed him, my rage was boiling, if it wasn't for a man holding me back and telling me to leave, I can't imagine what I would have done to him. Well, that is a lie, I've imagined it a lot since. While he was on the floor, the first thing I would have done is kick him right where it hurts. Twice.

Then when he was groaning in pain I would have knelt down, my knee on his neck, and pushed all my weight on it until he was running out of air, then released him and said, 'If I see you here again there won't be anything your Jesus can do to save you.' I've gone over it many times in my head. I think that is the best scenario, but there are others. Do you want to hear them?

Dr C: I'm wondering why this has caused you so much anger? There is a religious preacher not far from this room most days, you must have heard him many times, but never, to my knowledge, responded with so much emotion.

Eve: I can't remember any preachers. Plus, that was all Eve's stuff. Anyway, what the hell is he talking about? Doc, can't you see? Can't you of all people understand my anger? He told me *I* had sinned. I have done nothing wrong my entire life. I am not a sinner; I am nothing but a victim of sin. His God and his Jesus, if they exist, have caused nothing but pain and misery in my life and they dare to say I have done something wrong. *I* am a victim. *I* have been a victim my entire life. Can't you see it? Don't you agree with me? After everything I have told you?

Dr C: You have certainly been a victim to many terrible acts. Now I can see, Eve…

Eve: It is fucking EVIE!

[Silence]

I am sorry.

Dr C: It is okay. I can see how angry this has made you, and I can feel that anger too. Now tell me, what does "sin" mean to you?

Eve: What kind of stupid question is that?

Dr C: I know it may sound silly, just humour me for a minute.

Eve: Fine. I don't know... I guess, it is a religious word, that means doing something bad. Or, doing something that "God" isn't happy with. "What would Jesus do?" That is what they say, isn't it? As if he never did a bad thing in his life. Didn't he sleep with a prostitute? I'm sure I heard that once. Imagine that, Jesus actually had a child. He could have a relative on earth today. Imagine if he is some drunk, or a drug dealer. Wouldn't that be funny? Oh, sorry, sin. Right... so something Jesus wouldn't do? I don't know.

Dr C: So, that preacher telling you that you have sinned, is him telling you that you've acted in a way that would make God unhappy.

Eve: Yeah, that sounds right. I mean, if God is unhappy with me, then screw him! How dare he be unhappy with how I have acted after all he has done is destroy me? He wants to destroy me, punish me... torture me in every way he can and then tell me I'm not acting right. Well, I haven't acted at all! I have never done harm to anyone, I have never hurt anyone, I have barely even spoken to other people my entire life. How can you sin if you don't do anything?

[Silence]

I have been treated like crap my entire life, to the point where I have stopped bothering with all human beings. Just stopped talking to them, looking at them even thinking about them. Except you, of course. So, I've been persecuted for being alive and now I'm being persecuted for my response to that persecution. It's like, I get pushed and pushed and pushed into a corner, and then I crouch down and hide in that corner, only to get told off for not moving. Do you understand?

Dr C: I think so. It sounds like you can't win. What other options do you have, when you are in your corner?

Eve: That's what I am saying, I don't have any other options! I am forced into there and I can't get out. Aren't you listening to me? *I* am the victim! Why haven't you agreed to anything I have said? I am sick of this, you are just as bad as all of them, Doc, you know that? I thought you were supposed to support me, but you are just cold! You don't care. I don't even know why I bothered coming. I'm out, enjoy the rest of your boring life, Doc.

Dr C: I'll…

Eve: I don't care, I'm not coming back to see you.

Dr C: …keep your appointment next week.

Chapter 19 – Animals

'God, how do you do it?'

'Do what, sir?' the barman asked, curiously.

Brennan found himself in a bar he hadn't been in before. Attracted by its lights from the cold and dark evening, he decided it would be as good a place as any to resume his drinking. He was unsure how long it had been since he started drinking. Days? Weeks? It all seemed one large blur to him now. He thought, he mostly made it home at night or the early hours of the morning and did a good job of avoiding Amora at those times. Sitting now on a stool at the bar, sipping on some odd, sweet cocktail he had never heard of, he was observing the others. People sitting about, chatting about some mindless and mind-numbing topic – the weather, celebrities, television programmes, complaining about children, some guests even sitting next to each other whilst both swiping through their phones, as if the other person at the table didn't exist. The scene infuriated Brennan and, if it wasn't for the warmth, he would have probably left whilst sneering at all of their stupid faced.

'This,' he said, gesturing to all the other people, as if it was obvious, 'all of this. Doesn't it do your head in? You seem like an intelligent guy; aren't you sick of... the pointlessness of it all?'

The barman was confused but, being used to dealing with people after one too many drinks, he was well trained for the situation. He handed Brennan a water and, after saying "who are we to judge?", deliberately turned his back on Brennan and pretended to be checking the bottles of various alcohol placed against the mirror wall facing Brennan.

Brennan rolled his eyes in bored disgust at this comment. Either without realising the barman's obvious attempt to ignore him, or simply talking out loud to himself, he carried on. 'But look at them. Just look at them all. What are they talking about? It's just rubbish, dribble, is this the way to spend your free time? Sitting around talking about what celebrity has the best fake tits or who won some pointless game show? God, it just goes on and on and on. I'm bored... so bored! Is it just me? Is nothing popular exciting anymore? You know the Greeks used to sit around and talk about philosophy in their leisure time. They talked about truth, science, art, politics, things that matter, things that make a difference. What has happened to us? Honestly, what happened? You know what I think?' The barman turned around, assuming now that Brennan was talking to him, but the question was asked without aim at anyone and Brennan immediately answered it himself.

'The world is too comfortable, and we've regressed. We live so comfortably now, even people on the dole have a house with a fridge freezer, a flat screen TV, a laptop, an iPad, a garden, too much food etc. We are too comfortable now; we don't need to think about important things that actually matter. And so, people just don't need to *think* anymore… so they don't. They just sit in front of the TV and absorb all the crap it throws at them and just repeat whatever idea they heard last as if it was their own when, in fact, everyone else who also heard it spurts out the same nonsense.'

Bren had worked himself into a state now, getting louder and more animated. The barman looked at him suspiciously and Brennan, with a sarcastic smile and too much emphasis, took a sip of the water for him to see. Then he slumped back into his depression at the world and what it had become. He was simply bored of everything. His mind was numb with boredom. Nothing was interesting anymore and he hated anyone who thought otherwise. *Anyone who thought otherwise, didn't really think at all*, Brennan mused to himself.

'Animals.' He began again. 'They are just animals. Unconsciously moving about, driven by instinct and whatever nonsense all too easily brainwashed them. And they're happy. Happy idiots. Happy fools. If only they had an iota of intelligence, they'd see how pathetic their happiness is.' With this Bren downed the rest of the sickly-sweet cocktail he was drinking, and his face twisted into a grimace as the sugar coated his teeth and throat. 'You got any other disgusting mystery cocktails?' He asked with a smile.

'Disgusting cocktail coming right up, sir.'

'…better add a shot… of anything,' Bren said through a sigh at his own dreariness.

Observing Brennan, taking his time to mix together another of the most feminine of cocktails to his own amusement, the bartender considered what he had heard. His words made sense, especially for a drunk man. But here was this man, seemingly intelligent and thoughtful, he could surely take out anybody else in the place intellectually, yet for all his thinking and intelligence he was the glummest person this barman had ever observed. His conclusion was that this depressed man was intelligent in just all the wrong ways.

Bren downed his shot and as his head tilted back towards the earth, he locked eyes with another pair staring back at him in the mirror behind the bar. A young lady in a red dress had come to sit beside him. His gloominess immediately departed, along with his intelligence, which all made way for his instinctive animal lust.

Chapter 20 – The Trip

'Are we leaving yet?' Lilly's excitement was infectious. Joel didn't know what to expect from today, there were feelings he knew were bottled up in many of the locations they were going, he decided not to entertain them, but to keep them there until he arrived. However, excitement, he never thought would be a part of the day. Lilly brought that and she had enough for all three of them.

'Pack your sandwiches and your water and we'll be on our way,' Rayna said whilst using her hand to brush Lilly's hair off her face.

The two-hour drive to the first spot was filled with Lilly's games – I Spy, animal or vegetable, as well as her singing her favourite songs. Joel was grateful for the distraction from his thoughts. He was a quiet driver, always getting lost in his own head as the driving became almost automatic. In fact, he had some of his greatest ideas whilst driving, as well as some of his more fearful ones. As Lilly sang his mind took the opportunity to wander. It stumbled backwards towards memories in the dusty, cobwebbed crevices of his brain. It struck on the door entitled "school". Bursting open, Joel's mind was now flooded with recollections and the feelings they contained. Guilt, pain, embarrassment, excitement, jealousy, fear, lust, love, hope. How can five years of life contain such an infinite amount of feeling. The last five years of his life had flown by, memorable moments were barely a handful. Yet the five years of secondary school, it was almost overwhelming. He thought of his cockiness upon entering year seven. He was the king of his primary school and was expecting to continue that role in his new school. This confidence was quickly replaced with fear. It was such a big school, with so many children, some much bigger than him and so many were after the role he wished to fill. He shrunk in the face of it. The fear took over him now, almost as it did back then, thinking of those that jostled him, that made him want to cry, that made him cry sometimes, when they weren't looking.

His fear drifted away and made way for anxiety as he remembered the girls. Oh, the girls. He was mad about girls when he was in school. It was all him and his friends talked about. But he was also terrified of them. He was a coward, he thought then and still now. He would text them, talk to them online into the early hours of the morning, as smooth as you could be when you are a young teenager. Face-to-face, however, he'd get nervous. You see, online he could think about his responses, plan them, reword them, he was the master of

126

smooth talk. In school he only had his instinct to go by and it wasn't very helpful at all. It mostly told him to ogle them, to touch them, to kiss them. When it came to words and conversation, however, it wasn't interested at all. So, Joel had a series of never-ending relationships, consisting of online perfection and complete face-to-face awkwardness. The embarrassment coursed through his veins thinking about it and reddened his cheeks.

Then, however, came Rayna. She was in school the entire time he was, but she was never really on his radar. Until, one day, he happened to pass her music lesson and heard her playing Stealers Wheels on the bass guitar. He couldn't believe it, there weren't many people who liked his old school rock music, but here was a chance to talk to a *girl* about it. He had noticed her walking home from school a few times and waited for her to part ways with a friend before, not very discreetly, catching up with her. 'Hi,' he panted.

'Hi,' she said, giving away nothing but disdain and mistrust.

'I loved that song, Stuck in The Middle with You, right? Have you heard?' And that was that. Conversation after conversation about rock music, slowly turned into a romance, a love, a marriage, a life. What fate awaited him, he often feared, had he not gone to the toilet at that specific time and overheard the bass lesson.

Rayna held his forearm and stroked it with her thumb. 'Nearly there,' she said with a smile. Joel's mind shot back into the car. The singing that had been in the background of his thoughts had actually stopped; Lilly fast asleep on the back seats. 'All that excitement,' she chuckled. Joel turned the last corner and parked up just outside. The motion of the car that was rocking Lilly to sleep ceased and her eyes opened with a big yawn.

'Here we are,' announced Joel.

'Is that it?' asked Lilly, seemingly disappointed at their first destination.

'That's it,' Rayna admitted. 'Let's stretch our legs, take a look around.'

Leaving the car, Lilly stretched her whole body, reaching as high as she could towards the sky. 'It looks old.'

'It is old, much older than me and your mother. This is where we met, Lilly, inside these walls.'

'When you were at school?'

'That's right.'

'Eww.' Lilly laughed. 'Did you kiss at school?' She really did brighten their moods.

'Yes, Lilly, we kissed at this school, but only when teachers weren't looking,' Rayna responded, enticed by the thought of her daughter's childish disgust. 'And I used to think boys were icky just like you.'

They walked around the grounds of the school, now empty and quiet. Joel and Rayna reminisced about old friends, old teachers, their favourites and most disliked, events, memories. Lilly eagerly followed, enjoying her job as comedian and listening to all the old stories. *It was odd*, thought Joel, *most of his memories in school were charged with negative emotion, and yet looking back, discussing them with Rayna, gave them a new life, a new sense of meaning, a joyfulness even.* Each unhappy event, led him towards a certain direction, ending with Rayna and, ultimately, Lilly. Without anyone of them, perhaps, his life would have turned out differently. He was grateful for the bullies, the bad teachers, the detentions, the terrifying girls. Everyone was now a part of him, everyone played a role in influencing Joel's self, and things could have turned out a great deal worse.

Joel grasped Rayna's hand, fingers interlocking, as they headed back to the car. Lilly wouldn't be left out and grabbed her mother's hand. Suddenly, Joel released his grip on Rayna's hand and broke into a run.

'Daddy, where are you going?' Lilly enquired. On trying to release her grip and run after him, Rayna held her hand tightly.

'Don't you leave your mother,' she said and winked at Lilly. Lilly wriggled and jumped to get out of her mother's grasp, but Rayna grabbed her under the armpits and held her in tight to her chest.

'Let me go, let me go,' she shouted, whilst giggling. 'Where has he gone?' Lilly demanded, but with no answer.

Then, Rayna placed Lilly on the floor and said, 'Go on then, find your father.'

Lilly ran down the path of the school. 'Where are you, Daddy?' she shouted, giddy with excitement. There was a wall between the path and the pavement their car was parked. Lilly was gasping for breath as she sprinted down the path, she went to turn around the wall but suddenly screamed with terror and ran back the other way. For a second, she looked at her mother in fear, but her mother laughed at her. Then Lilly knew. 'Daddy!' she shouted, in joyful frustration. 'I know it is you.' At that moment Joel appeared from behind the wall with a large dragon mask on. Lilly stomped up to him defiantly. 'I can see you, dragon. I can see you, dragon. I can see you, dragon.' She repeated, with as much a courageous voice as she could muster, each time Joel physically shrinking into himself.

A brief ten minutes up the hill from the school was Rayna's parents' house. This visit, they both knew, was the source of Lilly's excitement. Rayna's parents embraced the role of spoiling Lilly rotten whenever they saw her. Lilly associated them mostly with hugs, kisses, sweets, cakes, fizzy drinks and games. Before the car stopped, it seemed, she was out of the car and sprinting to the front door. In years gone by her grandparents would have been waiting at the door to embrace her, but with their advanced age came first arthritis, then cancer, then dementia. They were stoic in their pains and Lilly couldn't notice most of their struggles. Using their spare key, Rayna opened the door for Lilly to burst inside and gently, as she had been taught, hugged her grandparents, both of which, held back their joyful tears of being able to see her one last time.

Joel always had great reverence for Rayna's father. Not the smartest man or particularly successful in his career, yet selfless beyond belief. He helped them with their first house, taught Joel how to be an all-round handyman. He had been a constant source of support for both of them and he loved Lilly no less than humanly possible. In his old age, Joel's respect for him only grew, as he dealt with his cancer with great courage and, now that it had been deemed unbeatable, he cared every minute of every day for his dementia suffering wife. If ever there was an example to follow, it was surely his father-in-law.

They drank tea and talked for hours. Rayna sought out old family albums and thumbed through the pages. Lilly delighted in seeing her mother as a baby and her grandmother as a young woman. When it was time to go, Joel or Rayna didn't have it in them to announce so. But Rayna's father sensed it and, slowly raising to his feet, he thanked them profoundly for visiting them. This time, although his face or voice didn't give it away, his sorrow was noticeable by the few tears slowly making their way down his face. For a long time, Rayna hugged him, expressing the million things she needed to say in the firmness of her grip. She kissed her mum on the head whilst holding her hand, and Joel shook his father-in-law's hand before embracing him.

As they drove off, Joel held Rayna's hand tightly. Lilly sensing their sadness, did an excellent job of making them laugh. Joel, however, only laughed shallowly, as his mind was in the next stop, his parents.

As the clouds gathered above, a wind picked up. Lilly started shivering in the cold and Rayna, kissing Joel on the head, took Lilly back into the car. 'We'll wait here for Daddy, okay?' she said, putting on the heating.

And so there Joel stood, staring at his parents' gravestones. Mr Carpenter, whilst cleaning the drive, slipped, hitting his head on the concrete, dying immediately. Mrs Carpenter's heartbreak killed her soon after. Joel remembered thinking at the time, how the simple knowledge of their presence before their death, was as comforting as the knowledge of their absence after was grief ridden. A bowling ball of grief sitting in his stomach, was how he once described it.

Joel sat on a bench overlooking their graves. It was a weird thing, as they were already gone many years, but now he was also approaching death, he felt the need to say goodbye to them. He wasn't sure what, exactly, he was saying goodbye to. To the graves, perhaps, to the memories that will no longer be in existence, more likely. He whispered at them with a croaky voice, his final goodbye. 'Thank you for all you have done for me, for Rayna, for Lilly. Thank you for your love, your care.

Thank you for doing the difficult things as parents. I owe you everything. We miss you every day... I miss you every day.' Joel sat in silence, trying to hold back his sadness. 'This is the last time I will be here and leaving now, is as hard as leaving the first time... I love you both.' With that, Joel wiped his face, composed himself and stood up. The cold had grown around him and, suddenly noticing the chill that had gripped him, he put his hands in his coat pockets and squeezed them into fists. Placing his mother's favourite flowers on their graves for the last time, he forced his eyes off their gravestones, and headed back to the car.

'Are you okay?' Rayna asked, waiting outside the car in the cold.

'I'm okay. Thank you.' With that they drove off, continuing their trip.

Chapter 21 – Who?
Where? What?

He was awake, slightly. The kind of awake where you hope, if you keep your eyes closed, you'll drift back off. But his headache wasn't allowing that, the thumping of it vibrating the bed, so it felt. A powerful, heavy thumping with every heartbeat. His head was bursting with pain and he could even feel it behind his eyes. He was still unwilling to move his head or open his eyes, for hope he can sleep through the pain. Between his cheek and the pillow was a dampness of dribble, caused by a night breathing through his mouth. He moved his feet first, moving them back and forth to feel the bed. The sheet was different to the one he was used to. Not a heavy duvet that his wife usually uses but a thin, light sheet. Yet the room still smelt of his sweat, it was a heavy smell, the type that needs a window opened, but Brennan was in no state to do so at the moment. His right foot moved backwards behind him and found the edge of the bed. He felt the coolness of the air outside of the sheet and the sensation gave him a momentary relief from his throbbing head. The dryness of his mouth spread down his throat and he craved water or juice, the thought was tantalising, if only he could move to acquire it. His eyes, too, felt dry and heavy. The thought of opening them brought a stinging sensation; it was no use.

Random flickers of memories from the night before came to him, not complete, but in parts. A song in his head, a smell, a feeling. The smell was a perfume, sweet, it filled his nostrils now in memory, the feeling, excitement, dread, nervousness, anxiety. They came back to him in bits, providing an incoherent story of his previous twenty-four hours. Then, the current feeling; guilt, shame, emptiness. It was in his stomach and chest, the heavy, emptiness of guilt was slowly overbearing him. He needed to get up, he needed to distract himself from these sober emotions.

The foot. It was still out of the bed behind him, free from the bedsheets embrace. He realised that he must have been on the left-hand side of the bed. His wife's side of the bed. She slept downstairs, he guessed. It wouldn't have been the first time in the last couple of weeks he'd found her sleeping downstairs. But he could sense her body, the way the sheets pulled at his skin, the slight sound of slow, calm breathing. She must have been on his side of the bed.

A bar, a waiter, a drink. A full memory came to him. Sitting at a bar, quite a posh one, he noticed, in his hand was a cocktail. He could taste it now, on the roof of his mouth and behind his teeth. The smell too, was noticeable, it wasn't welcome. Then a woman, a red dress. Just glimpses into the evening before he attempted to rid from his head. They were only adding to the feeling in his stomach.

The thirst was too much now, his focus moved entirely to heading downstairs into the kitchen and drinking a pint of water. He attempted with the left eye first. Opened it ever so slightly. It caused the thumping in his head to increase in intensity, but he persevered. It was open just enough for him to make out some rough shapes. His wife's silhouette under the sheet and further the light from the window breaching the curtains. The light from the window? It was as he feared. This wasn't his house and that wasn't his wife. Where was he? Panic started setting in. He needed to get up, to look around, to get some answers, but the thought of finding out more caused worry, could he just lie there and ignore it all? The panic filled his head and the guilt started filling his lungs. It was enough to make him cry. *Compose yourself,* he thought, *none of it matters, anymore, none of it.* The thought brought him relief. His mantra being now, "nothing matters anymore". He repeated this to himself until the guilt was pushed down and the panic left his head.

Both eyes opened now, the rigidity of his head and neck meant he didn't get a good look around the room.

But he could make out the woman now, next to him in bed. Slight, younger, thin. A feeling of achievement came over him. *Well done, Brennan,* he thought, *you've done well here.* This chirped him up somewhat. It was time to move, but slowly, not to aggravate the sledgehammer in his head. First turning his head, then body, until he was facing the ceiling. Using his arms and hips he got himself, slowly, to sitting position, his feet firmly on the floor. He was naked. He hadn't realised this until just now. A pang of embarrassment as he looked down at the grey chest hairs and beer belly sitting on top of his lap. His clothes were in reaching distance and he used his feet to slide them towards him.

Jeans and shirt on now, he felt a fraction calmer. His phone, it wasn't in his pocket. His eyes searched the room but to no avail. As the anxiety came over him, he recognised the feeling from the previous night. *Damn it,* he thought, *must have lost it somewhere last night.* His wife must've tried to contact him, even just a text, 'where are you?' It doesn't matter Brennan, he repeated, nothing matters.

Getting himself to standing, he turned to look at the random woman again. He assumed this must have been her house. She hadn't moved a muscle, still lying on her side, facing the window, facing away from him. He could make out her slow breaths as the bed sheet gently rose and fell. Part of him wanted to stay, maybe they could share the morning together, have a coffee, share funny memories of the night before. He chuckled at the stupidity of this thought. The disappointment he would notice in her eyes, the thin excuses she would use to get him out as quickly as possible. He was a pathetic specimen; it would take a terrifying woman who would be happy to see him next to her in the morning. He flirted with the idea of sneaking around the bed to catch a glimpse of her face. However, he decided, he was happy with how she looked from this angle, why ruin it, she could have a face as ugly as his. That would taint the memory for sure.

He settled on the idea of sneaking out as quietly as possible. So that is what he did. Finding his shoes, he put them on and stuffed the laces under his feet. He opened the door with the delicate attention of a spy. He took one last look behind, not a muscle moved. *She would never have to see what a mistake she made last night*, he thought. Gently closing the door behind him, he walked with more confidence into the kitchen. He checked the fridge. Orange juice, bingo! He downed it straight from the carton. His body rewarded him in feeling. It was cold, refreshing, clenched his thirst and loosened his throat. Brennan, leaving enough for the stranger to have half a cup, placed the carton back in the fridge and headed out into the world. He was excited, now, to discover where he was and what he was going to do next.

Chapter 22 – The Phone Call

The phone rang. It surprised Amora, knocking her out of a daze. She had been sitting on the sofa, staring at nothing for a considerable amount of time now. Lost wouldn't begin to describe how she felt. Her world had crumbled all around her, all at once, with a single news story. In this time, when she needed her husband for once, he was nowhere to be found. The news had knocked him out of a daze, but for the worst. She had only caught glimpses of him since the news. Hearing him stumble home in the middle of the night or slamming the door as he left the house during the day. He had disappeared along with her life. She was left alone, scared, in need of someone to talk to but no idea what to say. She pounced on the phone, a glimmer of hope. 'Bren?'

'No, sorry, it's not Bren, Amora,' the familiar voice responded.

'Oh, sorry. It's Thursday, isn't it? I forgot you'd be calling. How are you all?'

'We're doing okay, thank you. Is everything all right? Bren isn't there?'

'No, he isn't here. To be honest, things are not okay, I haven't seen him in days. Since the news he has barely been home. He's changed so much. He won't return my calls or messages. I even called his old friends, but they haven't heard from him. I don't know what to do.' Amora started whimpering, her voice was becoming muffled by sniffs and gasps for air.

'Amora, we're here for you, okay? I will try and find him myself.'

'Thank you. He never usually misses your Thursday phone calls. I know he isn't the nicest to you, but he does love you really. He just doesn't know how to show it. He used to be able to show it, to me, all the time. But ever since, you know, what happened with us, he has never been the same. This happened then, too, do you remember, but only for a few days. I was hoping that it would be the same, but this time he hasn't stopped, he hasn't come back.'

Amora's thoughts now rewound back to Brennan's turning point. She had composed herself somewhat during the phone call, but she lost control again now as the emotions came flooding back into the current day.

Amora was right. Bren used to be much more loving. Not the perfect husband, by any stretch, but he touched her, he hugged her, he kissed her passionately at times. Amora clung to that part of Brennan as it shrunk and shrivelled over the years, now but a leaf in the wretched forest of Brennan's soul. The turning point, she knew, was seven years ago. Nearly exactly, actually. She never forgot the date they found out. The pain and suffering, the heartache they both endured, the disappointment and feelings of uselessness, inferiority actually, came back to her now as the memories raced through her mind. In the doctor's waiting room, they were holding hands in the full knowledge and anticipation of bad news. They knew it was bad news, otherwise they wouldn't have been called in, but they didn't know the extent of it. Their names were called, and they were sent to room six for Dr Humphries. Bren released her hand and placed his on the middle of her back as they walked in. Then the doctor proceeded to tell them, carefully and honestly, that the problem wasn't just her and it wasn't just him, it was, unfortunately, both of them. They were both incapable of producing any children at all. She had Polycystic Ovarian Syndrome and Bren, basically, had sperm that wasn't up to the job. In the doctor's office, Amora managed to stay calm, and she asked lots of questions, none of the answers were what she wanted. There was, ultimately, no chance that either of them could contribute to child production.

Bren, on the other hand, was silent. He was silent in the doctor's office, silent on the way home and barely mumbled a word for days. He was broken. He was never interested in his job, or friends, or even his hobbies, but

Amora always saw the excitement in his eyes when they discussed children. After the news, Amora cried every night, she told her friends and eventually decided to talk to a counsellor recommended by the doctor. Brennan drank. Every night, more and more, drinking his feelings away. Until, eventually, he went out drinking and didn't come home. He was missing for a couple of days with only the odd message here and there to his wife. Eventually, his brother went out and found him. He was brought home and they helped him get off the drink. Since then, however, he was never the same. His brother called him every Thursday, at first to check he was managing okay, then it turned into a weekly chat. It gave Amora peace of mind to know someone else was checking in on him, although she knew Bren resented it and always saw it as an intervention. Bren was, after all, the older brother, and the phone calls made him feel like a child.

Bren's brother comforted Amora on the phone. 'The news has obviously hit him very hard. We'll get him back, don't worry. I know he has love in him, especially for you. Is there anything we can do to help right now; do you need anything?'

'You're so kind. Thank you. I will be fine. But, if you hear anything from him, please call me and let me know.'

Amora hung up the phone and made herself a cup of tea. She sighed a slight relief knowing she had support.

Sitting back on the sofa, she picked up her mobile, still no messages from Bren. She tried to call him again. Answerphone. She put her phone back on the coffee table, face up so she could see if it rings, and resumed staring at nothing.

Chapter 23 – Three Birds, One Stone

Eve: I'm sure you weren't expecting me today. I suppose I was quite harsh last week. I was just so riled up, you know? So annoyed. I'm sorry, by the way… I know you are only trying to help. You've been kind and, I've decided, I'm going to try and be kind back. It's hard though, being nice to people. It is a lot easier to just do what you want right? Do you know what I mean? Just, not care, what anybody thinks, or feels. Well, I can't be nice to everyone, I wouldn't get half the stuff I want done! But I am going to try and be nice to you. Try… anyway.

Dr C: Well, I am grateful for that, but understand if you get frustrated. This is, after all, a good place to get in touch with those emotions.

Eve: Yeah, don't I know it! So, last week, the religious guy, you were right there was a reason it was stuck in my head, a reason it annoyed me so much. I went back to see him, in the week, thought I'd try and talk to him calmly. It didn't really work though. When I approached, I could see the fear in his eyes, it made me feel so powerful, to have this man terrified of me. I couldn't help but play on it. As soon as he saw me coming towards him, he stepped off the bench and stopped preaching his nonsense. I planned on talking to him about why I was so mad and why he is wrong, I haven't sinned. But it didn't really happen that way. Not calmly talking anyway. I think I got some of my points across, a little more angrily than planned. His face just made me so angry, and he kept saying, 'You need to repent, you need to repent.' I could feel my teeth and fists clenching, I just wanted to punch him straight in the face. To be honest, I don't know why I didn't! I wish I did. I wanted to make him hurt, make him cry, make him feel for a second the pain I have felt most of my life. Anyway, it ended with me screaming, not words just a noise, in his face and then storming off. Before I left, I said to him, 'If God thinks I've sinned I may as well make the most of it!' And I have.

Dr C: You have made the most of it?

Eve: Yeah, like, if the big man thinks I am a bad person, I may as well be a bad person, right? Why not? So, I found out, finally, where my mum was living. I had it all planned out, everything I was going to tell her, all the ways she had let me down as a daughter, ruined my life, all the men she had brought home, the drugs, the alcohol… everything. I was angry and excited, like I was finally letting her know what she did. All these years she thought she had been a good mother and I was just a "weird" kid. She needs to know. Anyway, I went storming in there, but just I got to the entrance I noticed the man at the reception signing in. It was my dad. My actual dad. Remember, my real dad? Oh, Doc, that's when the rage really came over me. That druggy bastard ruined our lives. He ruined my life. He hit my mum, brought her drugs I'm sure, constantly left her and came back, never paid anything towards me. Never bought us food, never got me presents, never even hugged me. I knew what I'd do. I stormed to the car park, he always left his car open, I remember from when I was a kid, he never locked it, he always hoped it would get stolen for the insurance money. He probably had a new car by now, but I'm sure he still didn't lock it. So, I went through each one, one-by-one, trying the boot. Eventually, one clicked open, there was a golf club in it, I didn't think he was the kind to play golf… must have been a mid-life crisis. Well, I knew exactly what I was going to do. I took out the club, shut the boot, and let out all that rage. I smashed his wing mirrors, his rear mirror, his windscreen, I dented the car all over. And Doc, I've got to say, it felt great. I'm sure you wouldn't recommend it, but it sure was my kind of therapy. I felt exhilarated after. Like, I was cleansed. I thought of going in and seeing her, but I was out of anger and was afraid I wouldn't give her what I hoped. People started walking into the car park and so I ran off. Honestly, Doc, it felt incredible. I've heard there are these rooms where you can go and pay just to smash things up, like old printers and computers and stuff. Well, I can see the appeal! But why not do it for free with the car of someone you hate?

Dr C: Right. Well… I…

Eve: Oh, Doc, you are usually so succinct with your words. I've rattled you? Don't get that often I bet. Look, I'll keep going as there is some more, I need to tell you. So, I thought I'd keep sinning and ticking off that list. I knew it would work, the dress. It was red and very revealing, I heard red attracts. But, to be honest, I don't know if he was particularly picky. I'm rambling, let me go from the start. So, I put on a red dress. It wasn't mine, by the way, but that is another story. I went out to a bar, a fancy one. There aren't many open now, but this one was. I saw a guy drinking on his own and just thought, here's a chance, what have I got to lose? I sat next to him and asked, 'Are you going to get me a drink then?' I could tell he was already drunk. He got the bar man's attention and ordered me a champagne. Champagne? You know I don't really drink. He didn't even ask what I wanted, is that sexist? Just assumed I wanted it. Anyway, that stuff is disgusting. I had a sip and nearly spat it back out. I tried to drink it, I just kept pretending and tipping it on the floor, he didn't even notice. We talked, kind of. I mainly just flirted, touched his knee, his arm, I noticed his wedding ring. But, heh, I'm a sinner now, right? Two birds with one stone and all that. Before long, he was touching my leg, it was clumsy, I thought this would be exciting. It was boring, if I am honest. So, I just said to him, 'Are we going to have sex then?' He said it'll have to be my place, I didn't really want him there, but whatever. We started kissing, god it felt awkward, like sloppy, and his breath smelt of beer. After a while I had to tell him no more kissing. And we just did it. He got on top of me, but I don't think he was any good, I got on top, but I had no idea what I was doing. Then it just kind of fizzled out, I got bored if I'm honest. So, I got off, and told him I was going to sleep.

I never thought it would have been so boring… so awkward. His poor wife had to deal with that regularly! Or not, perhaps, if she was lucky. Anyway, I heard him wake up in the morning, I just pretended to be asleep, he shuffled around the bedroom, then left. I was terrified he was going to try and stay, that he might want us to spend the morning together. He didn't, thank god. The cheeky shit, I even heard him go into my fridge!

So that was it. Ticked something off my list, what a disappointment. Do you think I took advantage of him? He was clearly drunk. Maybe I did. Three birds with one stone in that case! Three birds, unmarried sex, with a married man, who I took advantage of.

[Silence]

Dr C: So, how do you feel, to have "sinned" three times in one night?

Eve: I thought I'd feel ecstatic, like when I smashed the car. But, to be honest, I just kind of feel dull to it all. Like, this was something I desperately wanted to do before, you know, the end. But now, it kind of feels like wasted time, like surely there was something better I could have done!

You know, time is getting on now, there's not much left. I'm starting to question my plan. Starting to question what I'm doing with what is left of it. Am I just wasting this time that's left? Is this really what I wanted to do with it? It's very confusing, you know. Maybe that is just Eve talking, maybe she's trying to slip through the cracks. She's been quiet for a long time now. Or maybe her bloody anxiety is just rubbing off on me! What are you trying to do, with your last days? I know you want to just tell me how to act… so what should I do with my last weeks? You're the professional, right?

Dr C: Well, we are all different. If you could go back, what would have been a better use of your time that night?

Chapter 24 – The News Part 2

The TV volume was way too loud, the setting left from the film they watched last night but being too lazy and intensely desperate to listen to what followed, they kept it blaring at them as if they were being told off by the man in the television.

"The rumours of the particular date and time have, now, been confirmed by the government's chief scientific officer. They predict, with, as we are informed, confident accuracy, that the asteroid known as Deimos will come into direct collision with earth next Friday morning, around 3 a.m …"

Standing up, mouth gaping open in disbelief, Wayne walked over to the television, turned it off, and immediately sat back into his groove on the sofa, giving the sofa only a momentary sigh of relief. He was stunned. Lost for words. It was quite easy, in all honestly, to stun Wayne and have him lost for words. But this was particularly unbelievable. The thought was only small and seemingly simple in its structure. *We are going to die, Thursday coming, at around 3 a.m.* A simple thought. Yet, at the same time, the thoughts meaning, what it entailed, was so incomprehensibly large and heavy, Wayne could barely contain it in his head. Attempting, futilely, to comprehend this thought, so heavy it seemed to way his head down onto his chest, Wayne became deeply, as deep as is possible with Wayne, upset.

'So... that's it then? We are going to die on Thursday? Everyone is going to die this Thursday?' Wayne asked, with open-mouthed disbelief.

'Yes, Wayne.'

'At *about* three o'clock? Just, *about* three o'clock?' Came tumbling out of his mouth.

'Yes, Wayne,' Janetta responded, again, as a robot.

'*About? About?* Could be two-fifty ... could be three-ten ... but there abouts?' He was talking to himself, ultimately, but he still expected, even needed, a response from Janetta. Her confirmation meant he wasn't going crazy. It meant he was actually in the living room and had actually seen the news he thought he had, not, as was certainly possible and, potentially, preferable, lying on a bed in, what Wayne called, a looney bin.

'Yes, Wayne. *About* three.' Now, Janetta responded, with a noticeable hint of agitation at his repeated questions.

'Bloody hell… bloody hell!' He became more animated, more upset, as he started to actually comprehend the thought. A moment of silence stilled the room, the heaviness noticeably darkened it. In that small moment of tormenting peace Wayne eventually managed to absorb the entirety of the thought. All of its implication started racing through his head, completely unable to focus on any of them, Wayne began to tear up. 'Why are you so bloody calm?' He raised his voice, tinged with anger and confusion.

Janetta deliberately accented every word of her response. 'I … am … not … calm … Wayne.'

Even he got it. She wasn't calm, in fact, she was using all of her will just to keep the appearance of calmness. She was potentially dangerously close to a breakdown, and Wayne's constant interruptions were not helping. He held his tongue. He sulked, as a child being told off. His chin resting on his chest, with his arms folded sullenly on his protruding belly. But he was unable to keep up the sulk for long, it was too shallow, too petulant given the news. His mind raced in every direction, incapable of keeping hold of any one image. It wandered into the depths of his past. His parents, school, friends he once had, the good memories with Janetta, the times he was embarrassed with how he'd acted towards her, as well as to the future, not something he often thought about, and all the things he will miss out on. Actually he thought, *oh, the things I will miss out on*. But he was unable to actually give any concrete examples of such things. Panicking, he wondered, *where were they going, what would their future have looked like, what had they actually done?* This was all too much for Wayne and, unable to hold his tongue any longer, indeed it had been nearly a whole sixty-seconds, the words came blurting out of his mouth, followed by a noticeable amount of saliva. 'We've had a good life, right?' His eyes locked hers, hoping to interpret her emotion from them. It was not as he was hoping. His best guess was disbelief combined with a sarcastic smile.

'A good life, Wayne? Ha! You don't half talk crap sometimes, but that is up there.' Her anger funnelled at him. Whatever a good life was, they surely didn't have it. *They barely had a life at all*, she thought. If their sofa were to disappear, it would at least be missed by them, but Wayne and her, well, there was nobody to miss them. Nobody would be worse off, without their presence. Who can live a good life and say such things?

Wayne felt a brutal pinch of emasculation at this. He had not provided his girlfriend with a good life. He had not even tried. He had never even thought up such a thing until this moment. And, at least, such harsh awareness, under normal circumstances, would allow him to change his ways, or at least the thought of changing his ways. However, there was nothing that could be done. It was all too late now. Wayne had failed. Failed as a boyfriend. His emotions clinging to this thought, he tucked his whole body in on itself and, with a feeling he hadn't felt since childhood, wept into his chest.

Initially, Janetta's eyes clung to her anger, she watched him weep pathetically, and thought just as much. But not for long. Her eyes softened quickly, as her maternal instinct took over, and she pitied Wayne and wanted nothing more than to comfort him. *The poor guy,* she thought. She was just as much to blame. She too had no goals, no idea of the future. She, too, would rather the pleasure of laziness in the present, than of hard work for the future. Jerking herself off the armchair, she sat on the arm of the sofa and embraced Wayne into her chest, kissing his greasy unkempt hair.

'I'm sorry, Janetta.' Wayne managed through sniffles.

'No, I'm sorry, Wayne. I didn't mean it. I am just angry at it all. You are right. We have had a good life. We've spent nearly every minute together. We've had no worries, no stress. We've argued, but we've always loved each other. That's got to be a good life, eh?' She was trying to persuade herself, more than anything, and even though she knew this, it was kind of working.

'Yeah… that sounds like a good life to me.' Wayne perked up, smiling through his sniffles up at Janetta. 'I do love you, you know, a lot.' As romantic and heartfelt a sentence as he could fathom.

At that moment, cradling Wayne's head in her breast, looking down on his tear stained eyes, his runny nose, his damp smelling clothes and tattered slippers, as he smiled hopefully up at her, lovingly, Janetta felt just like a mother. And that was always, unknown to her consciousness, exactly what she hoped out of a relationship. Wayne fit the bill perfectly. Perfectly, because, exactly what he desired, unknown to his own consciousness, was to be loved as a mother loves a child, no other kind of love would have done. Give Wayne romantic love, erotic love, fatherly love or childlike love and he will wriggle out of the situation as quickly as possible, as a worm in a bird's beak. No, it was a motherly love he craved and, in that way, both Wayne and Janetta were equally perfect for each other as they were the utter demise of one another.

And in this way, in this perverse yet, seemingly, functional relationship, they would both die. Wayne was born a child, obviously, but he never grew up. He was, unfortunately, born to a mother who loved her love, more than she loved her son. Thus, she refused to let him grow up, terrified by the notion that, one day, Wayne would no longer be reliant on her. Then who would she be, if not a mother? Then, not only could she be a permanent mother, but she also had the added bonus of being able to complain about it as if only if he would grow up, she could do all the things people would expect a woman of her age to be doing. And so, she suffocated Wayne with her love until he was utterly useless and pathetic, a child in an adult's body. And it was all futile, for Wayne naturally urged to escape his family home, as all boys do. Janetta, was a perfect replacement mother, allowing him to remain a child for the rest of his days. Once he had replaced her, Wayne's mother's demise was rapid and predictable to all who knew her, but it was no bother to Wayne, he needed her no more. And he will die never having known adulthood, in only a matter of days.

'I love you too, Wayne. A lot, a lot,' she responded, whilst stroking his warm, red, damp, chubby cheek with her thumb and smiling down on him.

Chapter 25 – A Car Ride

Joel skirted around the outside of the town, taking the ring road to the opposite side of where he lived and making his way in from there. The roads were eerily quiet, barely another car to be seen. It seemed, early on, very possible that the streets would be full of people losing their minds, looting, setting fire to anything, fighting etc. He had heard of it, on the radio and on television, in some other countries. Anarchy and chaos on the streets, citizens terrified for their lives. A part of him certainly expected such a scene here too, and he felt both happy and guilty that he had been proved wrong, people were dealing with this stoically, honourably, heroically even. Well, most people, anyway.

As he approached the centre of town, the streets too were deserted, except for the occasional drunk muttering to himself whilst stumbling on the pavement. Joel passed a keen eye over each of them. He remembered from before. Last time, he had travelled the length of the town looking, searching, fearfully. But this time he knew where to look. He was not fearful this time though, more pitiful. Pity wasn't an emotion he liked to entertain; it came with a certain bitter taste of patronising he disliked greatly. He resented his mind for feeling pity at that moment and pushed aside his thoughts to focus on the task at hand. No sign yet. He turned the car slowly down a one-way, cobbled street. Bars and pubs were either side, mostly closed, boarded up, but a few remained open. Possibly the owners wanted to drown their sorrows and allow others to join them. Or, possibly, they were part of the few who didn't believe in the news, thought it was all a conspiracy. He had heard their interviews on the news, and he couldn't help but understand the way their minds worked. How much sweeter their final days may be, living that lie.

His hand was outstretched on the stone wall of a bank, squinting into the distance with great focus, the focus of a man consciously trying to walk, like a toddler. His white shirt contained various stains, some rather peculiar, his shoes speckled with mud perhaps even drops of his own vomit as it bounced off the floor, and trousers, mud stained at the knee, fly undone and belt dangling down unbuckled. That was the target of Joel's driving. He pulled up beside the man, observing him for a second, expecting him to notice Joel there with the window open. For a second the man stood still, then, slowly, he twisted his neck to allow his eyes to gradually look up from the pavement, to the car, to Joel's face. His entire expression turned to one of pure confusion. If Joel was riding a space hopper, the man could surely not have created a face that expressed more confusion than his did currently. 'Get in, Bren,' Joel said, deliberately. Without a word Bren shuffled towards his brother's car, opened the rear door, and entered. Joel expected him to sit in the front seat, but it took Bren some effort to get into the car and he wasn't going to ask him to go through that again.

Bren caught Joel's gaze in the rear-view mirror. His eyes went from confusion, to understanding, to that of a defeated man, and he sobered quickly with each phase. He tilted his head until his eyes were focused on his shoes, allowing them to come clear in his vision as the alcohol gradually released its grip on him. Suddenly, painfully, reality set in. He had been here before, the reality was painful then but this, a second time, well, the pain stabbed him in his chest and how he wished, at that moment, that that pain would be enough to kill him. Everything he feared, despised about the world, in that moment, came true. Or, more correctly he knew, was made clear, for it was always true. And it was this; the world was wretched. It picked out Bren from the day of his birth and, for no reason at all, decided that this innocent baby would be the target of its torture. No matter how he fought back, with goodwill, with defiant happiness, it did not give up and wore him down little by little by little until it won. Bren knew it had won. He remembered that day, that day at the doctors with his wife, as the final masterpiece. Brilliant he considered it, perfect even, the final nail in the coffin was large, with a point as fine as possible and it was hammered in in one, brutal, unstoppable fist blow, right there in that doctor's room. That was the moment the world had won. Bren remembered the last rebellious thought leaving his head forever that day. From then on, everything around him available for his eyes to see, was a constant reminder that he was defeated, the poor chosen one.

Reminders really were everywhere, his work colleagues, the families in the park, his neighbours, the heroes on television. But only one reminder was worse than his wife. He knew she knew he was a loser, a defeated man. The way she looked at him, talked to him, touched him, even the meals she cooked him and the way she used to have sex with him. All of it indicated that she saw him as one who had been beaten to the ground and refused to stand back up, she pitied him, and that pity made him grind his teeth with anger. However, the one person who made him see more clearly than anyone, that he was a pathetic excuse for a man, was his brother. The resentment was so strong, he couldn't even look at him right now, as he sat in the driver's seat. You see, his brother was chosen too, by the world, but not to be defeated, but the exact opposite, to be carried over every obstacle that came his way. Joel simply glided through life, so Brennan thought, ever since the day he was born. He can even remember that day, when Joel was born, being four years older than him. Joel walked earlier than

Brennan did, he talked earlier than Brennan, he didn't have the eczema Brennan had, his teeth were straight, his hair thick, naturally thin and he quickly grew taller than Brennan too. Not only was this enough for Brennan to resent his brother, but his parents made sure he knew that Joel was fantastic, they told their neighbours, guests, grandparents, everyone they met, just how brilliant Joel is. Brennan knew, every time, that what they meant was "compared to our other son, Joel is…"

This moment, right now, looking at his shoes as his brother drove him home, nicely exemplified everything that Brennan hated about the world. Here he was, the pathetic, drunk, overweight, ugly, sterile, failure of a man and a husband, being driven home by the man who was everything he wasn't. All of his failures were sparkled, gleaming in his face, embodied by Joel. Joel, the man who looked after his wife, who had a successful career, who had friends, who gave money to his needing family, and who had a beautiful child. A girl. He used to think Joel saw him as equal, never pitied him. But since that girl, Bren knew that Joel laughed at him behind his back. How? Because Lilly, that sweet name, Bren had wanted to call *his* daughter. He had planned the name years before Joel had his girl, and he was certain, the more he thought about it, that he had mentioned this name to Joel, as the name he would eventually call his girl. Joel stole that name and called his girl it purely to throw in Brennan's face that he couldn't conceive. A spiteful joke, reminding Brennan that his dreams shall only be achieved by others, never himself.

The car rolled off, down the cobbled street and back onto the main road. Brennan's anger grew and bubbled over, with the target sitting only half a metre from him. The alcohol in his system gave him the courage, or stupidity, to confront his brother.

'She called you, huh? I thought she would… Joel to the rescue, eh?' His gaze not moving from his shoes. Joel considered Bren in the rear-view mirror and thought carefully about his response.

'I called her actually, it was Thursday yesterday, you know. I was expecting to get you,' he said with a calm and composure that only infuriated Brennan more.

'Ah yes, of course, Thursday. Your weekly phone call to check I am still sane. What luck I have you brother, otherwise I would be dead from alcohol by now. And Amora, well if you weren't calling every Thursday, she would be terrified, no one there to keep me in line! What a god sent you are to us both.' His sarcasm was clear from both the tone of his voice and the spiteful smile that accompanied it. Joel considered his options, after a small silence, he decided it best to not respond, not while Bren was in this state. No good was going to come from this conversation.

'Yes,' Bren continued, 'you are quite the hero. Always have been. You make the rest of us look like mortals. I can understand why they put up that shrine for you!' His voice was getting increasingly agitated, more excited, yet his gaze remained at his feet. Joel knew what he was referring to. His parents had had a number of pictures of both of their sons in their house, but on the mantlepiece there were six photos of Joel, some when he was younger, some older, some with his wife and child, all proudly facing the room with a couple of candles in between them. Joel disliked it. He learnt, over the years, that Bren was right, their parents had seemed to show favouritism towards Joel, and those photos were making it clear. Joel did ask, on a few occasions, for them to be taken down, but his mother would have none of it.

'The shrine to their pride and joy, the one they got right. From the moment you were born they always preferred you. Always! What the hell did I have to do to get their attention? The spotlight was always on you. You know how easy you had it growing up? I'm sure you don't as you've got nothing to compare it to. Well, I'll tell you, all your life you've had a red carpet rolled out in front of you leading to your next success. You haven't faced a tenth of the shit I've had to put up with. But there we go, you're the chosen one, eh.'

Joel kept his silence. He knew Bren was right, for the most part anyway. He knew his parents favoured him, but, if he was honest, he never considered to what extent. Even though he had always considered its impact on Bren, perhaps he underplayed its influence on him. Perhaps. But, come on, he is an adult now and has been for a long time. He's playing victim here, Joel thought, he's making excuses. He knew this, he knew his brother. He never applied himself, never attempted to exceed in anything and, although he certainly had more barriers to life than Joel did, Bren always seemed to hide behind these barriers and complain they were in his way. He never overcame them. It was all too convenient, and Joel was, he noticed, becoming frustrated with Bren aiming all this shame and anger at him. As if Joel was the cause of all his problems. As he thought this his face made an involuntary, inconvenient and provocative movement. His eyes, driven automatically by the thoughts in his head, rolled to display his lack of sympathy for Bren. During the silence, Bren took his own gaze off his shoes to try and determine what his brother was thinking. He witnessed this eye roll, and it brought a level of anger and contempt he had not experienced for as long as he can remember. The switch flicked and what little control he had had over his words was now gone, and out came the words in all their spite and venom.

'I know what you are thinking. That I am sitting here feeling sorry for myself. That I am being pathetic and weak. That if only I tried, I wouldn't be so bitter. Well that is an easy opinion for you to have. An easy convenient opinion for someone who has been handed life on a silver plate. You haven't tried for anything in your life, it's just fallen upon you. And you have the tenacity to say to me that I haven't tried hard enough?'

Joel nearly said, "I didn't say a word", but he held himself back – there was no use. Wishing he had not rolled his eyes now. But it was too late. They were ten minutes from his home, if he could get him there and have Bren run out of anger at the same time, at least, it would save Amora some hassle.

'And now this, this asteroid. That's it now, isn't it? It's too late now! The asteroid is coming, and you will die a hero, Joel, don't you worry, your fate is determined, you will die a legend. And me, ha, I will die a pathetic excuse for man. Never having a chance! This world, Joel, has ruined me! Shoved me into the ground repeatedly and now, it is ensuring it kills me in that state. As if there was a chance that things might turn around, it's finishing off the job. Control, that is all. It has had control over both of us! Don't you think you are autonomous, brother, you are just as weak as me. The only difference? Your fate was heroic, mine was embarrassing, both of us have been puppets so don't think you have done anything different to be in such a better position. Pure luck! Yes, you are just as weak as me. Feels bad, doesn't it? Good, about time you saw some reality.'

The car pulled up, eventually, outside Bren's house. Joel could make out Amora anxiously waiting in the window. She looked nervous, unsure of how to expect Brennan to be when he came through the door. Here, Joel made his final mistake, so it would seem. He couldn't leave Bren in this mood, what would it do to Amora. Putting his hand on the back of the passenger seat chair and turning his body around to look at his brother, who stared at him now directly in the eyes, rather menacingly, Joel spoke. 'I love you, Bren. It's never too late, you know, to make amends, to turn things around.'

'You're a patronising piece of shit, you know that? Without you to compare myself to my life may have been bearable. Thanks for nothing.' With that Bren swung open the door, stepped out of the car and, without looking back or saying another word, slammed it behind him. *Perhaps that was patronising*, Joel considered. He watched Bren walk towards the house and enter as Amora opened the front door. No embrace, not even a word was shared it seemed, Bren walked right past her. On the journey home, Joel reran the situation through his head, what should he have said? What would have been the right combination of words to calm his brother? None, he concluded, although this brought him no comfort at all.

Chapter 26 – The Bath

He walked straight up the stairs and into the bedroom, sitting on the side of the bed. A numbness came over him, he sat in pure silence, staring at the space between his feet. Even, now, his head was silent, not a voice, not a thought, not a feeling. In that moment Brennan had become a shell, inhabited by nothing. The occupier of the last month, that had been so emboldened by his drinking and reinforced by his recent attitude to life, had been quite exhausted by the car journey. It had run out of fuel. Tired, worn out, it took rest for the first time in a month and slept, leaving Brennan, in his current state of emptiness.

Amora was an excited mess. She was ecstatic he was home, in one piece. More than once had she considered that, maybe, he had died, been killed or took his own life, it wouldn't have surprised her, though it would have brought her unmanageable guilt. However, she was simply terrified by him. Not knowing him anymore. He was unpredictable. She was creeping on eggshells, completely unsure of what to do, how to act, what to say.

The fear of him leaving again, of her saying something and him storming out all over again, negated every idea she had. She remembered then his smell, as he coldly walked past her by the front door. It was harsh. A smell she would never allow in her home, in any other circumstances. Stale sweat, on top of stale sweat, combined with vomit and halitosis. She'd run him a bath, it was eventually decided. And get him a cup of tea.

After making the tea and running the taps, she nervously approached the bedroom. She could see him, sitting there, he seemed so small, she wasn't sure if he was crying or not. 'There's a bath running and a cup of tea for you, you'll feel better when you are cleaned up,' she said, with a forced bubbly tone. 'I'm so glad you're home.' No response, but that was as expected, she left the room, finished the bath, and went downstairs to give him privacy. Although, she listened intently from the bottom of the stairs. Not a sound, for the first couple of minutes, then a *creak... creak... creak* of the floorboards and a shuffling of feet into the bathroom. Amora filled with warm happiness. Whilst, Brennan bathed, she started cooking his favourite dinner for the both of them.

Stripped from his sticky clothes, Brennan planted his left foot in the bath, with no sensation, even his senses were numbed. Then the right foot. He stood there, for only a matter of seconds, as if he didn't know what he was supposed to do next, then it hit him. The sharp stinging circle around each calf and shin where the water surface met his body. It was too hot, agonisingly hot. It burnt. He put the cold tap on and gently shuffled his feet in the water towards it. Slowly, it cooled. He smiled. The nostalgia of all such memories came to him. She always made it too hot, way too hot, how she ever bathed in such temperatures he could never work out. He used to joke about it with her. She always used to run him a bath when he'd had a long day, and they worked too. She even used her scented bath bombs, he'd never admit to liking them and would even force himself to complain about them as he felt he should, but he certainly liked them, and she knew. *This one was mango*, he thought, the scent filled his nostrils as his calves had finally stopped complaining. He lowered himself, gradually, into the hot water, fully submerged he used his foot to turn off the cold tap.

He could feel the layer of, he didn't even want to know, shed from his body. He dunked his head under and rubbed his hair clean too. He took a long sip from his mug of tea; it clenched his thirst and cleaned his mouth. His rough throat was soothed with every sip. He was warm, clean, and he had a constant smile. Without a thought in his head, just pure sensation, he felt better than he had, not just the last month, but in the last year, two years, more? He looked his body over, it's new clean state, it was lighter, smoother, it looked like a different arm, a different leg. His hair felt fresh, soft on his head. And then that scent, amongst the mango, he could smell

Amora's cooking from downstairs, her love filled cooking. Then, finally, the thoughts filled up his head. *You fool, you idiot, you drowned me out, refused to listen, pushed me into a box. With your drinking and your hate, your anger, you almost killed me, and look what you got from it, huh, you became a smelly, lousy, resentful, homeless man. And all this, this heaven, was what you were missing out on. This is a normal day here, this cleanliness, calmness, warmth, this isn't a rarity in this house, it is every day. Why wouldn't you listen, why, on earth, did you throw it all away?* Bren had no answer, for the voice in his head. He just smiled and knew it was right. *But you are here now, it is not too late. Indeed, maybe, you simply needed to see the other side, to know what you were missing. Well you know now, the heaven you were throwing away. You fool. Your brother was right, though, and you know it, it's not too late to make amends.* With this thought, Bren relaxed into his body. All will be okay, it is not too late, even now it is not too late. He can make amends, he can appreciate Amora, again, she did love him after all. The love filled meals she made him, the way she always cared for him, the way she always saw right through to his loving side. He knew all this now, at once, and knew, also, that all of this had been tainted by his crooked mind. What excited him most, then, was the thought of getting out the bath, putting on fresh, clean clothes, joining Amora and hugging her, squeezing her, telling him how sorry he was, how he loved her, how lucky he was to have her, how he promised to live out these days by her side. In fact, he thought, *he'd promise to cook for her, to run a bath for her.* He'd make amends, or at least, try his best to. Thank god for his brother. He thought, *Thank god he didn't give up on me, that he found me, as before, and brought me home. Where would I be right now, if not for him?* The thought made him shiver all over and he discarded it from his mind. *I'll need to call him, too, apologise to him, thank him.* Brennan knew his brother would forgive him immediately and be happy for him. 'Ha!' he said out loud, laughing at himself. 'You've been a damn fool!'

Just then, rested from his slumber and awoken by the insult thrown at it of a "fool", the voice awoke and, having absorbed all that had happened, knew it could pop this pathetic bubble of ecstasy in a matter of words. In fact, it knew, this simple phrase of words will be all he will need to produce, and Brennan will do the rest with his crooked mind, no more will this voice need to contribute.

'And what,' the voice hissed in Brennan's ear, 'about the girl?'

Just the awakening of the voice was enough to tear Brennan from his state of bliss into panic and despair. *The girl?* he thought. *Oh, the girl. The girl with the red dress. Yes, well, what about her? It was a stupid thing, a stupid thing, there is nothing to think about. I will remove it from my mind. Amora? I can't bother her with that, these few days left, what would be the point? I'd tell her and then what, she'd be distraught? We'd fight, she'd cry, we'd die in agony, in arguments, in despair, that's no way to live out these last days. There's no need. Anyway, I don't remember what happened, who's to say anything happened? I have no recollection of the night.* A weak argument, Brennan knew. *Okay, fine, I probably did sleep with her, of course I did. I won't tell Amora, I will simply… I will simply…*

The voice was getting impatient now and was craving a beer, a whisky, anything to get his energy back. 'You will simply… lie? Way to make amends,' it added, sarcastically. *I can't lie,* Brennan thought, *I can't lie to her now. After all this, to lie to her and lie to her until our death, she would die a fooled woman. And I… I would die a fool and a devil. I cannot lie and make amends; I cannot lie and love her. Yet, if I tell the truth I will kill her, I will crush her. To tell the truth would surely crush her more than she had been these last weeks. Because, she would have been the idiot too, then, not only me. At least, when I was gone, she remained her dignity, that she deserved. The truth will make her die an idiot, but to lie would do so also. What have I done? I've ruined it. Ruined it all. I had this heaven, this home, but I didn't know. I threw it all away, for what? Pleasure? To live? Oh, you are an idiot, Brennan. You were living, your life was pleasurable, it was simply your attitude that wouldn't allow. You bitter, angry, self-righteous, superior arsehole.*

In that bath, where minutes ago warmth and ecstasy filled his veins and spread through his body, now despair and a hollowness consumed him. His heart seemed to recede to the back of his ribcage. There weren't butterflies in his stomach, but moths now, making him nauseous. He desperately wanted to cry, to sob into the bath, for Amora to come and hug him, her warm skin pressed against his. Even knowing it will be the last time. He wanted to feel her hands on his face, on his back, he wanted to touch her cheeks, to kiss her forehead, her hands, her lips. He wanted to stare into her eyes, to see her beautiful smile, to absorb her love one last time. He knew, however, that this wouldn't happen. How could this happen without him staying. He would never be able to leave, should he set eyes on her one more time, and to stay would be to ruin her. He wouldn't let himself consider Amora anymore, it was too painful, he knew what he had to do. As driven by a motor, Brennan left the bath, dried, put on his old, stale clothes, took money from the bedroom and headed downstairs.

Amora, excitedly, heard the footsteps. She was surprised how long he had stayed in the bath, but she assumed it was a good sign, he must have enjoyed it. Dinner would be about twenty minutes, but she had some snacks he could have in the meantime and she boiled the kettle again, to make him another cup of tea. The slow creak of the stairs and she was tingling all over, desperately trying to conceal her excitement, so not to scare him. Looking over to the bottom of the stairs, Brennan appeared, but in his old clothes. Without looking at Amora, he walked straight to the front door and left. Amora's heart sank, her tears came in an instant, she became hysterical. 'Please, Bren, please... not again!' She pleaded as she cautiously walked towards the front door. 'Please don't go... please!' She opened the door, her fears were correct, he was gone, nowhere to be seen.

Chapter 27 – The Sledgehammer

Dr C: You seem different today, Eve, subdued even.

Eve: I'm just so confused. Confused... about it all. Like my head is up in the air and it doesn't know where to land, it doesn't know how it should think about things. You know?

Dr C: How it should think about things?

Eve: Yeah... like... you know, I was shy and hid and pathetic and that wasn't any good, then I was the opposite, I wasn't anxious at all, but... I don't know... that doesn't seem to have worked either.

Dr C: Worked? How will you know if it worked?

Eve: Well, it's just a feeling, you know. Like... it'll feel right, or okay... it will feel like me... now I just feel like I'm faking everything... not being real... but I don't know what real is. Maybe I've never been real and over the years it has just faded until I can no longer find it. I'm left with just... masks, I guess. Trying to force each one on to see if it fits.

[Silence]

And now… I'm kind of… I'm out of time right? I thought I just wanted to have fun until the end, to make up for lost time. But what do I know, of what I want? I was wrong. I can feel I was wrong. I thought it would be so fulfilling, but nothing has been fulfilled. I still feel empty.

[Silence]

I went back to see my mum this week, back to the home. I think that visit was the cause of all of this… this confusion. I went back, I was angry and excited, to finally tell her how I feel, how she had ruined my life. I walked straight in, purposefully, you know, I was ready and eager. I went straight to the reception and asked what room she was in, that I wanted to see my mother. And… and… the woman stared at me for a few seconds, confused, and said that she was sorry, but my mother had died. She told me that she had died just last week, and they didn't have any contact details for me only for a friend. That's why he had been there, the other week, my dad, they must have called him in when she had died. I just stood there, staring at her. I didn't know what to do, what to feel, it was too overwhelming. After some time, she told me to follow her, and took me to my mother's room. It was still filled with all her stuff, not that I recognised any of it. But the smell, her perfume, I recognised that. I just stood there, stupid, and started to cry. The woman left; said she'd give me a bit of time. I became angry, I lost it. I felt like she had robbed me of the opportunity to tell her those things and that, now, she will never hear them. She will die not knowing what harm she caused. She will die happy, as if she thought herself a good person. The idea killed me, the thought of her happy. She didn't deserve that. I became angrier and angrier and... I just... I screamed until I was out of breath. Then I just started shouting at her, as if she was there, right in front of me. 'Don't you know what you've done?' I said, I was going mad, I was talking to the air, but I couldn't help it. 'Can't you remember? How dare you die happy?' I couldn't grab hold of any memories, but I had to tell her... so I just started rambling them off. The poor reception lady, I noticed her peek through the door at the commotion, but she didn't come in. 'You hit me, more than once. Slapped me across the face when I cried, when I was playing too loud, when I wouldn't sleep, remember? I saw you do drugs, all the time you did them, when you were supposed to be looking after me. And drink too. You were always drunk. I'd find you passed out on the floor some days. I was only a girl! You think that is anyway to raise a child. Don't you know what you have done to me? And the men... the...'

[Silence]

Sorry, I didn't mean to cry. I cried then too, whilst I was shouting at her. I was deranged, shouting at nothing. The whole home must have heard me. But I was just gone, I couldn't stop, I had no control of what I was saying it just came out. I kept screaming, too, in between sentences, deep angry screams, I have never made those noises before. I was terrifying myself. 'You used to bring back all sorts of men, remember?' I shouted. 'They'd hit you, beat you, get you in all sorts of states. I was just a girl. I saw you with black eyes, broken ribs, cut lips, a broken nose. Just a girl! I thought they were going to kill you. But you probably deserved it, what were you thinking? You were just as bad, you'd hit them, I saw you go for one with a knife, with a frying pan. Why did you bring them into the house? Why? You know what you made me? I hated myself, I still do. I was a weirdo in school, all the other kids used to make fun of me, I was so different. You know why? Because you were my mum... how was I ever going to be normal.'

I... I'm...

[Silence]

You know, I'm remembering it all now and, I'm sure, I am remembering it word for word. I'm going to go on, I want you to know everything I said. So, I told her, 'Do you know how I've lived? What I've been like since escaping from you? Like a hermit... like a nun! I'm terrified, all the time, and anxious of everyone and everything. I don't leave the house, I don't talk to people, I don't do anything. That's because of you... because of what you did. And do you know what I'm so scared of... I'm scared of becoming you! Of making your mistakes. Of being abused by others and myself. Of suffering constantly like you did and so I lock myself away and suffer all the same. And now it is nearly over, my whole life is nearly over, and it has all been misery and suffering. Why did you even have me? Why did you even give birth to me? Didn't you know that anything you attempted to raise would suffer so terribly? I wish… I wish I was never born!'

[Silence]

I… just need a minute. I said… I told her that and… and just fell to the floor, on my knees by her bed and cried. I was hysterical, I cried and cried… I couldn't catch my breath. When I tried to calm my breathing down, I looked for something to focus on and there, on the wall her bed was pushed against, was a picture of me and her, both smiling. I think it was on a birthday of mine, we were both wearing a cone birthday hat… you know ones with the string around your chin? Well, those. I must have been nine or ten. I looked so happy, a big grin full of baby teeth. And She did, too. I just stared at it, minutes went by and I didn't think anything. No thoughts at all. Just stared at it. Then… the words just kind of slipped out… I didn't think them first, they just slipped out of my mouth in a whisper, 'I forgive you.' I was surprised, shocked, I didn't know where they came from. Then I just started thinking about her, probably all the horrible trauma she went through with her mum and dad, all the things that made her, her. And, although I knew she was still to blame for much that happened to me, I did forgive her, and I felt it.

Dr C: You forgave your mother. What was that like?

Eve: It was… it felt… freeing. I had lifted a weight off myself. And you know what else? I didn't know who I was. I wasn't Evie and I wasn't Eve. I was just… well… I don't know. And thinking back now, it was like… I don't know who said those words "I forgive you", but it feels like at that moment that whole wall… remember the wall we talked about? It was like… that whole wall just tumbled to the ground, just rubble on the floor. And I've just been confused ever since… mainly… who am I? But I think… now… talking about it that that means that I am somebody… you know, does that make any sense at all? Like… because I am wondering who I am, that means I must be someone, right? Not just a mask.

Dr C: Because *you* are asking the question, there must be a *you*.

Eve: Yeah, exactly. Oh. Look, you've made me smile… you are good at explaining things.

Dr C: And the wall?

Eve: Yeah… I've thought about that. But, it has just all clicked in my head… just now. I told you before that the wall was created by all the people who gave me those horrible experiences, all the bullies and abusers and my mum and dad and… well… all of them. But I think… now… that… that's wrong. None of them could have built that wall inside my own head. Only… only I could do that. Only I could have built that wall. Why though?

I think… I was scared, I locked away any part of myself that could have resulted in me getting hurt, resulted in me feeling pain like I had or like my mum had. And as I locked it all up, I felt safe. But… I think… I also locked up a lot of good… a lot of parts that would have allowed me to be… well… happier. I built that wall. Yes. Yes… I built that wall.

[Silence]

Dr C: That seems like something of a revelation to you.

Eve: If only I had realised earlier… but then… maybe I would have never realised.

I know we are nearly out of time. But one last thing… you know… I don't believe in any of it… and I still think he was an idiot… but… maybe building the wall, locking away those parts of me, meant I couldn't do… well… anything. And maybe… that was the sin… the sin I committed… not giving my best to the world. Sounds silly, I know, it just kind of… came to me then.

Oh, I am sorry, I am crying now. This… I am not going to see you again, am I? This is our last session. You know, I don't know why you stuck with me, I really don't, I still think you must have better things to do in these days than see me. But I am so grateful you have still seen me, through all my silliness. How I would have died… otherwise. I'm just… I want to say… thank you is all. Thank you, doctor… thank you… Joel.

Dr C: You know, that is the first time you have called me by my name.

Eve: Yeah... I know... seems silly now. Thank you, Joel.

And with that Eve dashed at Joel and hugged him. Joel was shocked at first, but he embraced her and even cried himself, he was certainly going to miss her. She hugged him for well over a minute.

'Eve,' Joel said. 'I am grateful to you, for being so open, so honest, with me. You are the reason for your change, and I feel very grateful to have been a part of it. I am going to miss you.' And with that Eve sobbed and smiled. Thanked him, said goodbye, and left his office.

Joel sat there, for a long time, and just thought. So much had come to light in that session. *Why, only, in the last session?* he thought. Knowing, however, full well that it could only have been in the last session. He wrote his notes, collected his things, and headed home.

Chapter 28 – Possession

In the days that followed, a great battle ensued in Brennan's mind. He left the house knowing that he loved Amora more than anything, yet he also knew he could not see her again. To see her beautiful, love filled eyes would surely kill him. The sadness this knowledge brought consumed him quickly and he was desperate to be rid of it. He was desperate to feel anything else, even physical pain would have been preferable to the knowledge that he betrayed the most loving person he'd ever known. Indeed, physical pain would have been a release and he even found himself craving it at times. Some may have found him pinching his skin as hard as he could or kicking brick walls, even hitting his head against them, just to pursue the pain that overrides everything. Alcohol was the answer, he knew all along. There was that voice, that hissing voice in his head that urged him to drink, to forget it all. 'You'll feel better,' it said, 'once you have a drink.' Initially, Bren refused. There was something oddly addictive about this sobering suffering. In it, in his suffering, Bren remembered his love for Amora. Whilst he was suffering, he was suffering because he loved her and, he feared, if he removed the suffering, he would remove his love. He was right. It didn't take long for the voice to get what it wanted, and Bren turned back to alcohol to release him from his suffering. The voice won and it increasingly came to possess Brennan's mind with its favourite poisonous ideas. The alcohol knocked down Brennan's defences until he was almost entirely owned by these ideas.

The first idea, we know, was that nothing mattered anymore. This idea was so tempting, so tantalising, that Brennan almost willed himself to believe it. He forced the belief on himself and repeated its mantra until he believed it to be true. The idea possessed him to such a degree, that he would even brag to others, or simply to himself, about sleeping with the younger woman. 'What about your wife, isn't she upset?' they would ask.

'Well if she is, it won't be for long!' he would respond, laughing. The idea finally claimed his soul one evening when he spent a great deal of time staring at his wedding ring. It was dirty now, sticky on his finger. For a short period, whilst he was sober that afternoon, he had caught a glimpse of it on his finger and it overwhelmed him with sadness almost immediately. After a few drinks he brought himself to look at it again and, after some consideration, he took it off with his right hand and dropped it down a drain. He felt free, unburdened, released from Amora's love finally. He drank especially hard that night, with an extra chirpiness in his step. He passed out on a park bench in the early hours of the morning.

Brennan woke to shuffling feet and the sound of mumbling. He was freezing, shivering all over, trying to wrap his coat around his face and curls his knees towards his chest. He opened one eye, tentatively, to get a look at what had woken him. A woman was passing by, seemingly in a hurry, making tiny steps yet very quickly and muttering to herself. Brennan couldn't make out what she was saying, but she seemed rather happy with herself. She turned her head to face him, and Brennan quickly shut his eye so not to draw her attention. It didn't work, however. The happy woman shuffled over to him. 'Oh, you poor man… you poor man, why are you out here? You must have slept on that bench, but why? Do you know there are hotels here taking in all the homeless? Why are you sleeping out in this cold?' Brennan didn't answer and the woman gently shook him by his shoulder to get a response, he opened his eyes in irritation. 'Can I get you a hot drink, some food? Let me get you a drink, what would you like?'

'Urgh… go away!' He forced out of his lips with venom. The woman looked shocked and quickly shuffled off, still muttering to herself. Brennan uneasily sat himself upright on the bench. The day was too bright for his eyes to manage and his shivering from the cold had become painful in his jaw. Whilst considering what to do with his day the voice returned from behind him.

'Well, I am sorry, but I couldn't leave you here in the cold without anything. Here, it is a coffee, I don't know how you like it, but it's got milk and sugar in it, should help you warm up.' The woman sat next to him and handed him the coffee as if they were old friends. Brennan's foggy brain couldn't really comprehend all of this, but the steam coming out of the paper cup drew him to it and he took it from the woman. His hands warmed quickly and, for a moment, with the warmness and the aroma, it felt quite blissful. 'So, why are you out here? There are rooms for all the homeless now, don't you know?'

'I have a home,' he replied, holding his gaze on the coffee.

'Then why on earth are you sleeping out here?'

'That is none of your business.' He sighed.

'Well, fair enough, it is none of my business you're right. But… look, a man stuck his nose in my business once and it actually made a real difference. So… I don't know your situation, obviously. But whatever it is, it is not too late to change things. That is what he told me, "it is not too late". I'm sure you can change things around before the end, make amends. You see these?' Bren had noticed the jumble of thick blue and pink in her carrier bag. The woman took them out and showed Bren with delight, two knitted sweaters. The material was thick, and the sweaters looked shoddy, the arms weren't exactly even and were way too long for the size. But the woman seemed ecstatic over them. 'I made these, for my grandchildren. I have been a rubbish grandmother you know, a rubbish one, but I'm going to give these to them right now. Just in time. What do you think?'

'Just in time?'

'Yes, just in time. Don't you know?' She looked concerningly at Brennan. 'Don't you know what day it is? It is Wednesday.' Bren simply shrugged at this seemingly unimportant news. 'Wednesday! Tomorrow is Thursday. The last day. 3 a.m., they say. Three o'clock Friday morning, it'll… happen. You know I was very lucky to come across that man when I did.'

Bren understood now, what type of woman she was. He took a long sip of the coffee and looked at her for the first time in the eyes. 'You were lucky, eh. Aren't you lucky, you received that man? He came to you and saved you, you are fortunate! This world is not so kind to all of us. It is certainly not so kind to me! I have been born to be tortured by this world and there is no escape. So, take your knitting and leave me in peace!'

The woman started at this unexpectedly aggressive response. She stood up, but before leaving, told Brennan, 'I thought that, also, at times. It is just an attitude and not a helpful one… it is just an attitude.' With that, she left, still muttering chirpily to herself.

This was the second idea, that slowly possessed Brennan's mind. That he was being mocked by the world wherever he turned. No matter how he tried, the world always seemed one step ahead, ready to make a fool out him and at his pathetic efforts. He had a plan, one that had materialised in his head for some time now, of how to get ahead himself. As the days went on this plan made increasing sense to him. It now seemed the only way, the only way to beat the world. To have the final say. This woman, if she hadn't turned up, he may not have known what day it was. *What a fool*, he thought, *thank god for her*. With his plan solidified in his mind, he started the first phase, which was to drink. To drink enough to be able to carry out the plan, but not so much that he was incapable of doing so. Luckily, by now, he had become quite good at drinking.

Chapter 29 – The End Part 2

It was the night before. Wednesday night. Lilly knew, yet she lied in bed, excited for her bedtime story. Joel was still struck by her calmness about it all. He was sure she comprehended the situation, their fate, she had cried some nights and needed consoling, but on the whole, she had dealt with it so calmly she often made him forget about the whole thing. Tonight, she asked for his story about the princess, another one of her favourites. Joel read it to her, clearly and passionately. Initially he was struck by the realisation that this may be the last story he would ever read her. His voice was croaky as he held back the sadness, but he knew, if it was the last story, he would need to do a good job of it, and so he swallowed his tears and embraced the story.

...and after her husband died the Queen became scared of the outside world. She lost her trust in everybody, not even her most loyal servants and she ordered them all away, not to return. The Queen drew up the draw-bridge, she locked the castle windows and

put locks on every castle door. Only then did she feel safe. She took her daughter, the princess, in her arms and told her that she is safe, safe in this castle and with her mother, but outside these walls the world is scary, unpredictable, and if you venture out it will eat you up and spit you out just like it did to your father. The queen implored her daughter. 'Promise me, my daughter, promise me that you will never leave these castle walls, that you will stay in safety with me, so we both may live.' Her daughter obliged, and she promised the Queen she would never leave the castle. The Queen was happy with her daughter's promise. 'Oh the fun we can have,' she told her, 'we can play games, and make cakes and do all the fun things you love to do, so long as you stay here with me.'

And they did. They played games, they chased each other around the castle, they played hide-and-seek and "you're-it", and they baked cakes and stuffed their faces and had so much fun. One day, whilst playing, the princess was hiding in the large porch by the giant front gate of the castle. When her mother found her, she had a terribly fearful expression on her face, she grabbed the princess angrily and said, 'You mustn't go in the porch, it is too close to the outside, it is not safe! Do you understand me?'

'Yes, Mother, I understand, I will no longer go into this room.' The mother was happy and smiled at her daughter for complying.

But the Queen got more and more scared. One day, she caught her daughter skipping in the back room with its big windows opening out onto the garden. She grabbed the princess and dragged her out by her arm. She squeezed her daughters arm hard, until it hurt and said angrily, 'You cannot be in this room, it is too close to the outside! How don't you understand?' she shouted. The princess said she was sorry, but the mother was still angry. The mother got even more scared every day and, one day, in a frightful state, she dragged her daughter into her bedroom, threw her in and told her she must stay in there, for it is the only safe place in the house. The Queen bolted the door from the outside and hid in her own room.

The days went on and the princess would stare out the window all day, she was so bored. Then, one morning she woke, to a loud thud of wood on stone. She ran to the window, it was open, and she could see a large wooden ladder leant against her window, but there was no one in sight. She was scared someone would come in, but no one came near. She nervously looked at it for hours and, eventually, out of curiosity, she broke her promise and slowly climbed down the ladder. When she got to the bottom, she felt the grass under her feet, and the water of the moat, she heard the bees buzzing and watched the butterflies dance in the wind. She was safe, it was okay! Then she saw a bridge, placed down over the moat, yet still no one was around. She anxiously crossed the bridge and when she got to the other side, she heard the screech of her mother's voice. 'Get back here this instant! It is not safe, you will die. Get back here so I can lock you up in this room, I will put bars on your windows and chains on your hands if I must, to keep you safe!' she screamed at the daughter, but she couldn't go back, she needed to explore and she told her mother she loved her and walked into the world.

The princess found that her mother was right, the world was cruel, harsh, unfair, painful and it brought death. But her mother was only half right, as the princess learnt. The world was cruel and kind, it was harsh and soft, it was unfair and fair, it brought pain and pleasure and it brought death but gave life. The princess never went back to the castle, even though it contained no death, it also contained no life, and now she loved living.

'The princess is so brave, like me, right, Daddy?' Lilly asked through a large yawn.

'You are very brave, Lilly, just like the princess.' He kissed her on the forehead. 'Now goodnight, sweet dreams… I love you.'

'I love you,' she responded with a big smile.

He thought, on this night, he would never be able to sleep. Peculiarly, however, a great tiredness came over him that was so overbearing he barely made it to bed before falling into a deep sleep. Then it was Joel's turn, to sleep and to dream. As soon as he slept, he also woke, so it seemed, into this now familiar place.

He looked down to his feet, the thick hazy blackness of the air fuzzed his view, but there he could see them on the tracks. Impenetrable blackness filled all around, side-to-side and above, the only thing visible was the tracks, which ran on infinitely into the distance, fading into the dark. The air was cold, but it was not biting as usual, it felt fresh on his skin. His senses felt sharp, clear, as was his mind. Joel was come over, not by a sense of panic, or the unknown, but by a sense of purpose this time. A feeling of great understanding sat in his head and seeped through his body. Not physically, or visually, but in some other sense Joel felt above, abstracted from the whole scene, he was at once both a purposeful participant and an observer. Although, if asked, Joel could not at all articulate these feelings, nothing in this dream before had felt so real.

The familiar vibrations started, the small stones and scraps of metal and splintered track leapt off the surface a centimetre in the air as the knowledge of something approaching, something big and from behind him, was clear. He breathed, deeply, and although the vibrations increased, his feet stood still, strong, firm to the ground. When before the urge to look behind plagued his mind, now simply an understanding that he *must*, was present. The pain, the inevitable pain, caused a wince at the thought. He had felt it many times now, the screaming agony of his neck and spine as he grinded the vertebrates together to twist his head behind. His hips pleading as he forced his legs, so slowly, to face back. His whole body pierced with agony, bringing his body to sharp breaths and the need to curl into a ball on the floor. *Brace yourself*, he thought, *a deep breath and here we go.*

First the head, he closed his eyes ready, and began to twist it. He opened his eyes, and his head was twisted as far back as it could be. No pain, he moved smoothly, as if his whole spine had been oiled. He twisted it back and back again. Relief. Joy even, at the great pain he had been spared. Then the legs. Again, they moved smoothly, easily, his joints had been greased. His whole body moved to face behind, so comfortably, he performed the whole movement again. There, deep into the distance, were the lights, making their way towards him, the bringer of the vibration. They reminded him of his purpose, and he turned around and headed off, forward.

As the vibrations increased, his legs, nevertheless, passed over each track firmly, lightly, it was as if he was almost weightless, gliding over the tracks. Joel's gaze, fixed firmly forward as he strode in the direction of the tracks, was lit up ever so slightly, but increasingly, as the light bounced off the steel and into his eyes. The vibrations increased, the light increased, his sharpness and purpose increased as he kept a steady pace. The sound that broke the silence was not from behind, but from in front, somewhere in the darkness. It was breathing, heavy breathing, the sound of a man running. Faintly at first but it grew closer and louder with every step Joel took. The man was out of breath, clearly, struggling to fill his lungs enough to keep him moving at such a speed and the sound of spluttering and failing lungs was clear. In fact, it was right in front of Joel now, a sound with no owner, as he heard the breath in his ear and then it passed. The sound was running towards the lights, sprinting in fact. Joel became overwhelmed with panic now, worry, and as he turned to follow the sound, only part of him knew what he would see. It seemed, part of him knew this was exactly why he was there, and yet another part was completely dumbfounded, shocked and terrified and what Joel now saw, the owner of the sound which had now taken physical form. The hair, the back of his head, the body, it belonged, without a shadow of a doubt, to his brother. Yes, it was Brennan. And Joel watched, with disbelief, as Brennan sprinted towards the lights, desperately trying to keep his footing amongst the vibration of the tracks.

The panic that overcame Joel in his dream state, only increased upon sharply waking. Automatically, his head turned to check the time, 2:40 a.m. Something was wrong, he could feel it and knew where he had to go. Rayna woke as Joel was changing. 'I need to see Bren… I can't really explain… but something is wrong, I can feel it.'

'I'll come with you,' Rayna responded, alarmed by her husband's state of frenzy.

'Stay here with Lilly, I'll be fine.' Just then, a feeling possessed Joel's mind of such sadness and suffering that his heart sunk, and he almost fell. Rayna noticed it, in his eyes, the way they stuck to hers and became vacant, for only half a second. Joel tried to shake it out of his mind, but a remnant remained, souring all his thoughts. 'I'll be back as soon as I can... I love you.' These three words were delivered so deliberately they seemed to transfer that possessing feeling to Rayna's mind also.

'I love you too,' she said, through watery eyes, as she hugged him tightly. Joel squeezed her hand and kissed it before leaving the room. On his way passed he creaked open Lilly's door and observed his daughter sleeping, for a few seconds, absorbing her entire presence. Then he left.

As he drove, this thought of what lay ahead of him plagued his mind. So dire and saddening was it, that it urged him to turn around and return home, to his family. But, alas, he could not, he would not. For his brother was his family too, and he knew his brother was now in need. The road ahead became blurry through his tears and he wiped them away with trembling hands. It was a ten-minute trip and he thought of Rayna and Lilly the whole way there. He thought of hugging them, kissing them, their sweet, beautiful smiles, the warmth and joy they brought to his soul. He considered all this, causing his face to become wet with his tears, whilst his heartbeat raced with anticipation.

No light was on in the house, he could see this from the outside. But he was drawn in, he knew Bren was in there, his whole being knew it. Shaking, his hand brought the spare key up the front door and slowly, quietly, twisted it unlocked, pushed the handle, and entered the house. He was drawn through the hallway, the kitchen and into the living room. And there, sitting on the sofa, with a cushion sandwiched between his head and a gun, was his brother.

'Bren, it is okay. Please don't… put the gun down… you don't need to do this.' Joel tried to find the right words.

With surprise, Bren turned to see his brother. It was all too much, too confusing, his brain couldn't keep up with the thoughts, the feelings, everything that was happening all at once. His face maintained his confusion as he stared into his brother's eyes, yet the gun remained in place. 'Let's talk, okay… let's talk about this… put the gun down, please,' Joel almost begged as Bren's face remained mixed in confusion.

What happens now? thought Bren. *This wasn't part of the plan. I should be dead by now. But there is my brother. How did he know? Why did he come? He's been crying, it was clear from his red eyes. He's here for me, to stop me. But, how did he know?* Bren's thoughts whizzed through his mind, too perplexed to grasp anything at all. *Slow down,* he urged his mind, *slow down! He is here, in front of me, my brother, asking me to stop. Asking me to not kill myself. He knew, somehow, that I was doing this, right now, he knew, and has come to stop me. He cares. He cares? He must care, but why? Why care, now, what the hell does it matter? Only a day before we all die anyway. Is he right to care? But it is clear that he does, he really does… he cares for me. Huh… I don't know why,* Bren considered as his thoughts slowed to a snail's pace*, but he cares.* That thought lingered in his mind, as the gun began to drop from his head.

Creak… creak… creak. The sound came loudly, quickly from upstairs. Down came Amora, rushing on the stairs to find an unimaginable scene in front of her. 'Bren!' she screamed. 'What are you doing?' She was panicked, she looked at Bren, she looked at the empty vodka bottle, the notes, the gun, it was clear to her immediately and yet it seemed so inconceivable. 'Oh my god! Bren…' she stammered as the realisation set over her. She wanted to run over to him, to grab the gun out of his hand, to hug him and tell him she loved him. But there was a part of her that was terrified of him, utterly. She didn't know him anymore. The man that was her husband had changed rapidly and horribly over the past month, who was this man, could he shoot her? Could her approach cause him to shoot himself, as he so clearly intended? It was only then, that she actually noticed that the other man in the room was Joel. With the panic and fear she grabbed him, her arms around his neck she cried into his shoulder. 'Help, please help,' she begged. Joel didn't hug her back, his eyes remained fixed on his brother's. He saw it in his eyes, the thoughts were so clearly translated into his brother's face, Joel watched it all, as clearly as if they had been read out loud to him.

What is she doing? Bren thought. *Why is she hugging him? After all this, he is the one who gets her attention? Why, is it always him? Why?* His thoughts screamed at him now. *Just when I thought he had come to rescue me, he had actually been sent to mock me, one last time. To mock me as he has forever. This perfect man, this hero, this ideal has come to make sure I am blinded by his perfectness one last time. To ensure I know how useless I am, how much I have screwed things up. Not I! It! The world. How much I have been cursed by this world and, as its last act, it's beautifully wretched finale, it makes me look upon all-that-I-am-not just one last time. If it had been a second later that he arrived I would have been dead. Peacefully dead. The timing was too perfect, the world sent him to mock me, it wouldn't even let me have this in peace. Now I have to look upon it, with my wife draped over it, the one who makes me look like a pathetic excuse for a male. I won't be won over, I will not let this wretched world have the last say, the last mockery. I will finally have my say! Here is what I say to you, world!*

The thoughts went by in all but a few seconds, but Joel read each one of them, and as the tears left Joel's eyes and he thought of his Rayna and his Lilly, he felt the bullet pass through his chest, as he knew it would. Then he was on the floor, awkwardly, for a second, then two, then three, then he was no longer on the floor, but somewhere else entirely. In fact, by the time Bren had turned the gun onto himself, and, whilst crookedly smiling at his defiance over the world, then ended his own life, Joel was standing once again, face-to-face with the vast emptiness.

He saw in front of him how the lights and tracks were consumed by the emptiness. But he was calm now. He pushed his hand through and, although cold, it was not freezing. With the lingering, warming thought of his family, he said goodbye to both and followed his hand in and through. And as he disappeared into the void, Joel's body's heart stopped beating, its lungs stopped breathing, its blood stood still in its veins, and, with a final breath, he died.

Chapter 30 – The Neighbour

She knocked on the door, quite nervous, but excited, also. She could hear the slow shuffling inside. 'I'm coming… hold on,' croaked the old, withered voice. She waited with anticipation. She was bound to be surprised at her presence. A lot of planning had gone into this, she prepared what was in her hands with great care and effort, just for this moment. To give back. To show her appreciation, her kindness, her caring nature, all of these attributes she now knew and was so excited to explore them, to see what they did, how they acted with the world around her. Where they would take her, into the unknown which, although still anxiety provoking, now also provoked great excitement and curiosity. *Shuffle… shuffle… shuffle*, she was at the door. The sound of the door chain being pushed to the side, the clanking of it dangling, the click of the lock being undone. The excitement was bubbling up now and she had to contain herself. The old woman slowly opened the door, raised her head at the unexpected visitor and gasped. 'Oh… well, this is a surprise… ha! What a lovely surprise…

and what have you brought? Oh… I have to say you have never looked so beautiful… what a lovely surprise… how unexpected! Well, please, Eve, come in, come in! I'll fetch us some tea. Come in!' Eve's neighbour was as giddy with excitement as Eve was.

Eve walked into the house, quite amazed by everything around her. It smelt quite musty, like old carpets and old wood mixed with rose perfume. The neighbour had not stopped talking to Eve, or just to herself, Eve couldn't quite tell. She took the baking tray from Eve. 'And what is this? Well… it looks like lasagne. Oh, what a fabulous treat, I'm looking forward to having this tonight, what a lovely treat. Please, dear, come into the living room, make yourself at home, I will just fetch us some tea.' Unsure what to say in such situations, indeed she had had very little experience, she just grinned warmly at her neighbour.

Upon entering the living room, Eve looked around. Everywhere there were photos. On the walls, on the fireplace, on the windowsill, on the chest of drawers… everywhere. Stooping down, Eve looked at each photo intently. Some of her neighbour in her youth, with her husband on their wedding day, abroad, some of them with a child, some professional and some spontaneous. She looked intently at each one, enjoying the thought of her neighbours full life. The things she must have seen, experiences had, a life lived to the full.

'Ah, yes, beautiful, aren't they?' her neighbour said, warmly, whilst bringing in a tray with an old-fashioned tea pot, pot of sugar and milk with two cups and saucers. 'That one, that there is my husband and my boy, beautiful eh? Of course, they are still with me, I talk to them in those photos every day. They talk back mind dear, don't think I am crazy now.' She laughed.

'They are gone?' Eve asked, knowing the answer. She also realised she hadn't spoken a word since entering the house and thought, in these situations, that people do probably talk.

'Yes dear, both died. They were on a motorcycle trip together, touring around France. A terrible accident, both died. Over two decades ago now, how time flies. But, as I said, they are still here. Those you love never leave you.' She paused for a second, smiling at Eve and analysing her face. 'You do look very beautiful you know, have you done something with your hair? Please, do sit down. You know it is so nice to see you, I do worry about you, you know, all alone over there. Yes… sit right there dear. Here, I'll pour you some tea, you take sugar?' And without time to answer the old woman tipped in a teaspoon of sugar and stirred it into the cup, so excited she was to treat her guest. Eve just smiled and nodded at her. Eve was enjoying herself even more than she had hoped. 'I know a thing or two about being alone, about being lonely. I have been here for a long time by myself, not a soul to talk to. How nice it is of you to come and check up on me. An old woman like me, you must have better things to do.'

'No,' Eve managed, unable to control her happiness as a large smile appeared revealing her dimples. 'There is nowhere else I'd rather be. You have been so kind to me, I only wish I could have returned the favour earlier. You really do have a lovely home.'

And with that Eve and her neighbour talked and talked. Well, the neighbour did most of the talking, but Eve could not have been happier to sit back and listen. To drink tea with someone, to sit in someone else's living room, to have someone smile at her, Eve nearly cried with her joy. "You must have better things to do." The sentence from the old woman hung in Eve's head, how many times has she said that or thought it? She laughed at herself. *Others feel that way too? Maybe I am part normal after all.*

The evening drew on and Eve was so engaged with the conversation about her neighbour's family, their holidays, their games and so much more that she barely noticed the time pass. They even shared dinner together in the end. Not once, Eve noted, not once did they mention that this was their last day. They never mentioned the asteroid that was hurtling towards the earth. *Did she know?* Eve wondered. Well, of course she knew. Eve was happy to not mention it and have, what she assumed, was a normal evening with a friend.

'Now, Eve,' said the neighbour, using her arms to push herself up to standing. 'It has been such a pleasure to have you over, I don't get many visitors, you know. But I am an old woman and very tired now from all this excitement, I must go up to bed. I am so grateful for your visit, so very grateful. What a joy!'

Without thinking, Eve walked towards her and, gently putting her arms around the old woman, hugged her tightly. 'Thank you,' Eve whispered into her ear, 'for everything.' Holding the old frail woman in her arms she could feel a tear drop onto her dress from her neighbour's eyes. Releasing her but keeping her hands on her shoulder, she said, 'You know, at times, you were the only kindness I ever experienced. Thank you for letting me into your home. Goodnight.' Eve warmly smiled at her.

'Goodnight, dear.'

With that Eve left and slowly made her way back into her own home, contemplating something all the while.

It was late, and Eve made her way to the bedroom. In full knowledge of what tonight was, what would entail during the early hours of the morning, Eve still had all intentions of sleeping. In fact, she felt she would sleep tonight better than any other. In the face of this, her last night, she had such a feeling of calm and serenity, even contentment. Without knowing what she would say, Eve knelt down at the side of her bed, and with her hands pressed together, fingers interlocked, and her chin delicately placed on top, she began to pray. If Eve was honest, she knew not what she was praying to. She wasn't even completely convinced it was God. Maybe it was some other higher power, or perhaps to fate, or even simply to a part of herself. She didn't dwell on this, it was unimportant, even if it was only to herself, she needed to speak, to say the things that were now so coherent in her mind.

'My life has been hard. Much suffering and pain and anxiety. I have locked myself away and spent my life in fear. Fear of feeling pain again, of being hurt or betrayed by others. But my fear only brought more pain, more suffering, but at the hands of myself, I just did not see it. And now this, this impending death, this inevitable fate. It has forced me to face it all, and I have. In giving me death, you have given me life, if only for a day. But to live for a day is better than to not live for an entire lifetime, this is what I have learnt. I am grateful, for the lesson, and, I am grateful for today.'

With that, Eve got dressed, looked out the window, up at the great ball of light hurtling towards the earth. Shut her curtains, and fell into a deep sleep, of which she never woke.

Chapter 31 – Two Letters

Amora sat on the bathroom floor, she was unsure how long she had been sitting there. She was out of tears, her throat was dry and hoarse, she could feel its raw pain every time she swallowed. Her mouth was dry, eyes stinging and heavy. Hours had been spent, trying to bring herself to read them. She noticed their scruffy handwriting and the crispy patches where tears once fell. She brought Joel's up to her face first, with trembling hands, and began, finally, to read.

To my brother,

Joel, my brother, how I have hated you over the years. I have despised you, passionately. I know now, why. I have always told myself it is because you have been so lucky and I so unlucky. That you have had everything handed to you in life. Mum and Dad favoured you so much, I know you know it too. I used to think you loved it, relished it, held it over me as a sign of your dominance. But I know, now, in this brief moment of clarity, that I am sure will not last long and thus, why I have decided to write these letters now, I am sure they will be read before the end, I know that none of this is so. Looking back, I no longer see your enjoyment of Mum and Dad's favouritism, but I see your guilt. The look in your eyes when they did such things, your awkward looking at me, you wished they hadn't done so. You would try and make them see me the same also, I used to always find that so patronising, but I know that it was in a good nature. I have never visited their graves; did you know that? If I am honest, I didn't love them for a long time before their death. I know you did, I used to hold that over you too, but no longer.

But not only parents, life as well, has treated you so kindly. I think that this is because you have embraced your fortunes, whereas I only ever compared mine to yours. My mentality has always been that my fortunes fell so short of yours, everything you had was better than me. Your wife, your child, your job, your books, your money. It made me hate it, that jealousy, it blinded me to what I had. I have a wife; a loving, kind wife, I had a good job, we have enough money, we have a nice home, but I didn't see any of it, too blinded by jealousy. Without being able to see it I slowly undid all the work that got me there. Until I was miserable, bitter and angry at everything, but you, you were always the target of that anger. I wish now that I had talked to you more. You called me every Thursday, without fail, I hated those phone calls. I always thought they were patronising.

Now, I wish I had embraced them, I feel like now I have so much to tell you and yet I will probably never speak to you again. I wish I had visited you; I was barely ever at your home except when Amora dragged me there. And when I was there, I was quiet and moody. I wish I had visited more, especially to see my niece, Lilly. She is a very beautiful girl and so funny. You know, the fact that you could have children was the final straw for me. How petty, that I hated you for it. Pure fortune. Just chance, I hated you because of chance.

Twice, you have saved me. Twice! You left your family and searched for me, picked me up and took me home. I remember, both times, I hurled abuse at you, told you what I thought of you. You never got angry at me, I even hated you more for that, for not getting angry. If only I had the ability to perceive your love. Well, I am writing this, now, not long after you have saved me for the second time and brought me home. I was going to stay, but decided that I cannot, due to my actions. But I want you to know that I appreciate how much you have done for me, and for Amora, where would she be without you.

As I am writing this, I am daydreaming of being able to see you, to hug you, to thank you and tell you I am sorry, I do love you. To see your family and smile and laugh and be a brother-in-law and an uncle, what a treat to be an uncle to that girl and I've thrown it away. But I have made my bed, there is no going back for me now, I cannot explain it to you, I don't think you would understand, but I must lay in the bed I have made.

I love you, Joel, a great deal. I am afraid, before long, this feeling will have left my head and I will return to my bitter state. But I need you to know that I love you, I appreciate you and I am so grateful to be your brother.

Bren

Amora read this, silently, hearing Bren say every word and feeling every one of his emotions. She understood it all, she had always known how he felt. She had always known, too, that he had this love inside of him. *If only he could have read this,* she thought, *all of the things that could have been.* She tormented herself, as she had so repeatedly that day, with what could have been. *If only,* she thought, *Bren had considered the letter he had written before using the gun, if only I had approached him, showed him my love not my fear, if only I had removed the alcohol from the house.* All the possibilities every last detail whirred around her head again and again, as if she thought, coming across the right detail to change, would alter the course of the past. But she only punished herself with such thoughts. What she was really doing was procrastinating, avoiding reading the final letter, the letter addressed to her.

Placing Joel's letter back on the floor, she grasped hers and felt the paper, imagining Bren's hand doing the same. With her head facing the ceiling, she placed the letter in her lap and leant it against her legs, with her back pressed against the cold tiled wall, taking some deep breaths failed her, as the fearful anticipation made her breaths short and sharp, as if she was crying without tears. She tilted her head down, daring to look at the paper.

To Amora, my beautiful wife…

'No, no, no, no, no, no,' she repeated. 'I can't… I can't do this.' Amora wailed these words, or something unintelligibly similar repeatedly. It could have been minutes or hours before she plucked up the courage again, so was the concept of time in this desperate sadness. She managed a deep breath and focused her eyes again on the page.

To Amora, my beautiful wife,

When I think of all the misery and upset I must have caused you over the years, and especially now, I tremble with anger at myself. The thought creeps into my head all the time and I constantly push it aside, too scared of how it will make me feel. What it tells me about myself. You are, without doubt, the kindest, most forgiving and loving person I have ever known. It's why I fell in love with you. I couldn't believe my luck when you agreed to go on a date with me, kissed me, agreed to marry me! I know I have shown that to you less and less and less as the years went on. It must have seemed like I was torturing you, making you seem worthless to me. When, actually, it was the complete opposite. I was lucky to have you, but that was just it, I wasn't good enough, I didn't deserve you. That is definitely true, I did not deserve you. And that is how I felt, like I wasn't worthy, like you'd be better off with someone else. I know how you think, please don't blame yourself, it is nothing you did or said, there was nothing you could have done differently, it is purely a terrible attitude on my behalf. My terrible, bitter attitude. I knew I wasn't good enough, and I knew I never would be, it was an impossible task. I started imagining you with someone worthy, imagining you enjoying yourselves, having fun, someone who could make you feel loved, like I thought I couldn't. It plagued me, this thought, and it went around and around in my head until I believed you dreamt of it too, of someone worthy of you. Although, I know that that isn't how you think and I know, I knew deep down, that you wouldn't have dreamt of another man. But I am weak, and pathetic, and I was jealous of this man I had made in my head.

The truth is, now I think about it, that I just didn't love myself. I loathed myself, hated myself, thought I was the worst of men. I wore myself down so much that I just gave in to it, accepted the person I thought I was. You know, I hated myself so much I wished at times I didn't have to spend every second of the day with myself, it is a weird thought I know, but that's how I think.

Now, I am in our bedroom, after just taking that bath you ran me, and I can smell your cooking wafting up the stairs. All I want to do right now Amora, all I want is to come down those stairs, and squeeze you and never let go. To squeeze you and tell you I am sorry, sorry for how terrible I am, sorry for not being the husband you deserve, for causing you pain and misery. And tell you that I love you. I do love you, Amora, so much it hurts all the more. Then we would sit down and eat your beautiful cooking together and snuggle up on the sofa and talk and watch a film or something, I miss those days so much. I never made the most of them, of that time with you, how lucky I was to have all that time with you and how terrible I am for throwing it all away.

But I cannot. I cannot go down and see you now. You see, I have insulted you beyond belief. I see no other option now, than to go. I have been so awful to you and I cannot do so for another second. Yet, what I have done. I must tell you the truth but cannot be with you once you know. Amora, in the state I have got myself in over the last few weeks, I had sex with another woman. To the woman who has given me everything, I have thrown it all back into her face. For that reason, I cannot stay. If I stay and tell you the truth, you will undoubtedly forgive me, and you will die being a fool who wasted her love on someone who was unfaithful and I would know it and see it in your eyes every day, yet if I stay and lie I would do you only more dishonour and deceit, which would eat away at me every second. This is why I have to go.

Amora, while I am thinking clearly, I need to tell you that no man would ever be good enough for you. Yet, I didn't even try to be. Your love was so pure and perfect, all I wish now is that you know that I loved you with every part of my being and when I allow my thoughts to wander they imagine how things would be, if I could turn back the clock and start again with you. I would try every day to be the man you deserve.

I love you, I love you, I love you.

Bren

Amora's eyes found new tears and they streamed down her face now. 'I love you, I love you,' she kept repeating. She read the letter again and again and again. Each time her thoughts punished her with what-ifs. What could she have done differently? And Amora read and cried and thought and read and cried and thought until her brain could take no more. She curled up on the cold bathroom floor, shivering and whimpering until the end, which wasn't so far away.

Chapter 32 – The Dragon Part 2

It was Thursday evening. Joel had left with such a panic and with such words that Rayna had feared the worst. Now, with him not returning and no answer at Bren and Amora's house, Rayna could only suspect the worst had happened. She could not leave Lilly, but she also couldn't take Lilly with her to find Joel, what if they found him as she feared. Rayna had been panicked all day, pleading for him to come through the front door. This wasn't how it was supposed to end. Lilly had asked her where her daddy was and Rayna could only answer honestly, 'He needed to see Uncle Bren, I don't know when he will return.' Now it was evening, and she knew he wouldn't return. He had seen something terrible in his sleep and whatever it was, Rayna thought, it had come true.

She was the one, now, who had to have this conversation. She was the mother, the only parent in the house, and she had to talk to Lilly about what was coming. She entered her room and disturbed her daughter whilst she played. 'Lilly, I need to talk to you.'

'I know, Mummy,' Lilly said, with a playful air. 'I know you need to talk to me about what is coming.'

'You know?' Rayna responded, confused.

'Yes, Daddy told me we would have to speak about what to do with the last day. It is the last day today. But I already know what I want to do.' Lilly's words were so matter-of-fact, so stress free that she took Rayna off guard.

'You already know?' She responded once more, still confused.

'Yes, Mummy, we need to be brave. We need to face the thing in the sky. We need to look at it and see it and be brave,' Lilly said, as if it was obvious that was what they must do.

'So… you want to look at it?'

'Yes.'

'Okay, if that is what you want then that is what we shall do.' Rayna was so surprised by Lilly's casual manner, by her smiles and joyful expressions, that she really was unsure if she comprehended what was happening. She wanted to keep things normal for her, as much as possible, until the end. 'Dinner will be ready soon; I've made your favourite.'

Lilly and Rayna ate their dinner and played games until the sky became dark and they both sensed what was coming. Lilly took her mother by the hand and led her outside. The asteroid was huge and bright in the sky, clearly moving now, its sight made Rayna shudder and her hand started trembling. Lilly held it tightly.

'I wish Daddy were here.' Lilly sighed, for the first time sounding sad.

'Daddy is here, Lilly, he is here with us, he is always with us.' Rayna tried to reassure her daughter. She got down onto her knees and took Lilly by the shoulder, looking her deep in the eyes. 'Lilly, you are so beautiful, so funny and kind. I am very lucky to be your mother, I love you very much.' To hide her tears from Lilly, she immediately embraced her and tightly hugged her.

'I love you too, Mummy.' Lilly replied warmly. They held each other for minutes, feeling the movement of each other's chest with each breath, feeling the warm air pass by their ears. Rayna kissed her daughter on the lips, then on the head. Lilly could see her now strained red eyes. 'We need to look now, Mummy, we need to be brave.' With that, Rayna stood up, not letting go of her daughter's hand and they both stared at the asteroid hurtling towards them. Rayna could make out Lilly gently whispering, with a shakiness to her voice: 'I can see you, asteroid. I can see you, asteroid. I can see you, asteroid.' Lilly repeated over and over. Her courage was so impressive, so inspiring Rayna felt comforted by her own daughter. She felt stronger, able to stand up straighter and join Lilly in her courageousness. And together they chanted until precisely 3 a.m. when it all came to an end.

In her small life, Lilly had learnt more courage than most, and she faced death as courageously and bravely as she would have faced the life she was losing. In that way, perhaps it could be said that she died well. Perhaps, even with nobody to know or remember, this was important.